Juliet + Juliette = Love in Mafia Land

J. S. Nathaniel

Published in
Denver, Colorado

JULIET + JULIETTE
LOVE IN MAFIA LAND

Copyright © 2025 by J.S. Nathaniel

All rights reserved. Except for brief quotations in a book review, you may not reproduce or use this book or any part of it without the publisher's express written permission. **No AI Training.** The author reserves all rights to license all uses of this work for generative AI training and development of machine learning language models.

Because the planet is quark size, if one can reach another solar system with a copy of this book and desire to share, then the author gives their blessing. By then, the author would have perished in an untimely fashion and wishes you Godspeed.

ISBN: 978-1-967522-00-2 (Paperback)
ISBN: 978-1-967522-04-0 (Hardcover)
ISBN: 978-1-967522-19-4 (E-book)
ISBN: 978-1-967522-02-6 (Audiobook)

The legal department recommended that the author reveal content warnings:

The construction of this literary piece harmed no unicorns or three-headed blue thumpers. Although, the title is implicit. Mafia Land murders fictional characters on the daily.

This is a world of fiction. Nothing more.

If the reader bumps into Leonor Saramago in the real world, then you're double fucked. Outrunning Leonor is fruitless.

"Persons and images depicted are models and used for illustrative purposes only."

Also by J. S. Nathaniel

Contents

For the Lion's Gate Portal, WR 102, Iota Cancri, and UGC 9273.

Narrator's Note

The reader will soon discover a travelogue. These literary markers are at the end of each chapter. Not every creature or mystical insect will go along with a travelogue. All epic journeys intend to leave the reader a little wonder. As the narrator, I will not think for you, Uncle Stigmata often said. While we're discussing Uncle Stigmata. I must legally disclose, it will be a bumpy ride. When I say bumpy, I mean bloody. Fear not, the suns eventually tower the dark. Let us not forget, this is a tragic tale, but a love story at heart.

Thread of Love

THE DAY HAD FINALLY ARRIVED. But did she have the guts to execute the plan? A plan that would destroy Mafia Land and rid the world of Mother rule? A plan cooked up four years ago, on the nose, by Uncle Stigmata? No, she was not fearful of what lay ahead. Not a smidge. Could she stomach what she was about to do to blabber-mouth Devin? Yes, sadly. When evil crawls inside the heart, there's little that can be done.

She flicked a finger in the air and instructed the squad to raise him higher. Meeting eye to eye was paramount. Especially when delivering a fatal message. An eye relays something words cannot, Mother Saramago would say, if she were here to see this event. But Uncle Stigmata would advise, aim for the throat—the quickest way to stop the heart.

She stroked his cheek. Pathetic, clammy tears soiled his skin. Her eyes were vacant, as though Devin were taking part in a schoolyard game. Then she thought, *Devin isn't here anymore. Not dangling by a thread. Not screaming his pretty little head off.* Rather, he traded places with a baba foot and was now caught in a snare, waiting for the meat grinder.

His pale arms stretched toward the rafter like a rag doll. Hands purple and bound with hemp-lock rope. Bare feet swaying above pavement. She placed her lips to Devin's ear and whispered, "This is goanna hurt." He smelled the platinum elixir swim from her breath. That intoxicating smell traced back to the House of Saramago.

Devin's muffled scream blasted through the gag. She touched her lips. "Shhh." Her eyes softened like unicorn eyes. Her face angelic. The glint of the snips stung his eye as she placed sharp steel to bare nipple.

He didn't scream this time. Instead, he muffled nonsense. Tears pouring down his face. His body trembling.

"Say it." She shoved those snips in his face. The steel somehow gleamed in the dull light. Snip, snip.

Devin nodded. His eyes were desperate, as though drowning.

Leonor ripped the gag from his mouth. He screamed again. "Uh-uh." She waved the snips in his face. "The simple part is over."

"It wasn't me."

"Spill it."

Devin shut his mouth and refused. She motioned to the squad again. They hoisted him higher, causing the last drop of blood to settle in his toes.

He howled from being stretched to hell. Through the heartbreak whimper, he said, "Juliette."

She lashed out her hand. The high school point guard, Remedios, lowered Devin to eye level. Leonor's eyes changed gears. Maybe frightened to hear the truth. "Juliette," she said, "Juliette Marquez?"

Devin saw shock take over her face. It seemed to shatter every bone in her body. Love, perhaps, was what pained her so. But he couldn't be sure. He lowered his head and sobbed. "Yes."

The squad gave Leonor the told-you-so look. Remedios peered at Leonor. Those haunting eyes pierced her twisted little soul. "Juliette Marquez is next. Blood in, blood out."

Remedios glanced at Lia, waiting for her to agree. Lia nodded with disgust. They settled the matter. The squad had agreed. Juliette Marquez must die. Except Leonor imagined her heart was now dangling alongside Devin. She wasn't mentally ready for the truth. For Devin to blurt Juliette's name. Her mind went elsewhere after that. She was no longer in the room. Not on the same ship. If a ship existed.

"No!" Leonor turned her back on the squad. Now she was the desperate one on the hook. She stood there searching for the right—no, the perfect—thing to say. Anything that would stop Uncle Stigmata's plan from unraveling too fast. She felt vengeful stares burn a hole through her. Even poor Devin was giving her that look. Compressing her to the ground. "Killing her would start a war."

"Last time I checked, the Mothers were at war," Remedios said. "She killed Tetchy. A made dude."

Leonor sunk her nails into Devin's face. "Liar."

Devin looked up, defeated. "I saw her do it, I swear. We snuck into the rager."

In his terrible confession. Under intense pressure. He forgot to mention that Juliette had accidentally killed Tetchy. The smoking gun was in her hand when the damn thing went off. Juliette had tried to stop Tetchy and Juliet Saramago from fighting over a kiss. Devin later called it a "Silly kiss," considering Juliet and Juliette were from rival houses. Instead, Juliette had punched Tetchy's clock at one sharp. Something Devin should have had the balls to do. The bullet could have hit any of them. Though luck dined on Saramago blood that fateful night. The bullet punctured a main valve. He bled out in seconds. Juliette tried to stop the bleeding, but it sifted through her hands like a bargain-basement elixir. The circle of life. A gangster life. Here today, sure to bleed out tomorrow. Or maybe the next.

The loud music drowned out the gunshot. It wasn't until the rager had ended and the lights had burned bright that someone stumbled upon his lifeless body. Blood jutting forward. Well, all over the place. A mafia-style hit. Blood for days. Weeks after that, to lift the stain from the stone floor.

"See," Remedios said. "How would he know Tetchy was at the rager?" Devin spoke the truth for the first time in his miserable life. No one dared speak the truth while dangling on the hook. Except for Devin. Today, a perfect storm was spearheaded by none other than Devin Marquez. *What a little shit,* Juliet would scream once his confession traveled throughout the land and made its way to the House of Saramago.

Leonor could not cover her tracks now. Not after Devin spoke the truth. She never dreamed Juliette had murdered Tetchy. It made perfect sense. Juliette Marquez crashed the party and masked herself as a plague doctor. But why, Leonor wondered. A plague doctor christened the moment. Everyone in Mafia Land knows the plague doctor ushers in the apocalypse. It mattered little which side people chose. Both sides would drown in blood.

Did Juliette Marquez crash the rager out of infatuation for a boy, or perhaps was it a girl? Infatuation makes fools of us all. Enough to crash a party behind enemy lines while being outnumbered. Now she thought, *Who is Juliette's love—enough to crash a rager for?* Leonor needed to spin this the right way. She needed to find out how infatuation turned into a love bomb. Before time ran out. A love that soared to the stars. A love that led to her destruction and ruin Uncle Stigmata's plan.

Two major events happened at the Baroness Mansion while peeling back the thumping music—a love connection and death. Love chased death. As it often does in Mafia Land. Juliet fell in love with Juliette. They kissed passionately, but brief. Seconds on the seconds. Which turned into dope-sick love. They swam in each other's eyes. Lost elsewhere, just the two. Yanked from a land of violence. One tiny push toward something brighter. Hard to see what lay ahead. Where to go from there? Heart palpitating through all chambers. A rush of zinger blood. The smell of whipper sweets. Juniper swimming in her mouth. The sweet bite of true love.

They swore an oath to each other, sealed with a kiss. Not a pinprick. Not blood to christen the moment. Not a card of saints set on fire. Then passed down from hand to hand, as the ancients did. A lock of hair not required. The world belonged to them. Everything else vanished. A brief encounter proved enough. No longer searching. No longer lost. Juliet lived a lifetime in those seconds. Two hearts swam as one in a sea of deadly uncertainty.

Juliet decided after the kiss. After she savored the juniper that rubbed off from Juliette's tongue. She would no longer marry Sebastian from the Carlito House to settle Mother's ambitions to one day rule a nation. A marriage that would unite two powerful families. Instead, her heart now belonged to Juliette Marquez of the Marquez House. A rival house. A long history of bloodshed between the families. Where love, death, and fate would unite again in the darkest way possible. Yes, ultimate destruction was looming somewhere over the majestic mountain scape. She didn't care about the consequences. Juliet was in love with Juliette, and that was that.

They say love knows no bounds. In Mafia Land, people often frown upon love. Noted as a diseased heart.

"Cut him loose."

Remedios and Lia looked at each other. Then sharpened eyes on Leonor. "He'll warn the others."

"Yeah, especially Juliette."

"I will deal with her my way."

Those were the truest words ever spoken. Leonor had no intentions of harming one strand of hair on Juliette's head. Unless it benefited. She took no joy in delivering death notes. Despite her assassin ways. Her two-headed sphinx eyes. Nothing-scares-me attitude, as long as death didn't somehow merge in the same sentence as Juliette Marquez.

Leonor knew timing was everything. At least Uncle Stigmata seemed to think so. If Juliette should meet a premature death, the plan would unravel faster than a zigzag doing light speed in a twenty.

Travelogue

The *baba foot* is a velvety creature that fits in the palm. The baba foot, a mountaineer at heart, lures the two-headed sphinx from crystal caves. The two-headed sphinx has wandered off with children from nearby villages during the winter months. So, there's that. Meal preparation for a baba foot is simple—meat grinder. The meat is so dry and tough it requires tenderization. Which raises the question, why eat something that will shatter teeth?

The *zigzag* is a fascinating creature. It's the fastest insect on the planet. Not a soul in Mafia Land has captured one in over a thousand years. It lives so long it's almost immortal. Even death can't catch it.

Zinger blood is a rare elixir made from the carcass of a zinger. One of the slowest creatures on the planet. Which has baffled scientists for years. Not the slow part, but its strange molecular reaction on the human body. Why does the zinger give whoever consumes its flesh a rush of energy?

Secrets Wilt Like Tiger Petals

THE HOUSE of Saramago held every dark secret the land could ever hold. Indoctrinated by the Vatican method. Even though Leonor and Remedios were not Saramago by birthright. They refused to let Tetchy's murderer escape justice. Remedios demanded an eye for an eye. That's the only way to right a wrong.

Under certain conditions, water doesn't always freeze. Nor does it conform to the ways of a mighty river. Sometimes water finds another way around the problem. So much so, it carves another path.

Mother Saramago lay in a luxurious spa filled with platinum elixir. Juniper and whipper sweets moistened the air. Mother's head leaned back against the rim. Steam cobwebbed. She wore a mask of gold. Roots from the purple wisp covered her eyes. Hands caressing cold hammered copper. Her body floating in bubbling water like spices in a cauldron. The hum of the jets was at full throttle. Leonor stood at Mother's right. Remedios at her left. Both girls wearing bitchy faces. Sinister smiles for days.

"Mother, I came as soon—"

Mother raised her hand and removed the purple wisp. Then glared at Juliet. That look transcended words. "Is it true?"

Juliet was speechless. Her face already told the story. Mother was better than a lie elixir. One glance, and she could read the truth like a fable. "To be honest, Juliet," Mother layered the purple wisp on her eyes again, "I never cared for Tetchy. He was my brother's little prick. He was always stepping into shit wherever he roamed. I knew one day a jealous lover would punch his clock. I'm surprised he lived this long."

Juliet had been holding her breath without realizing it. That stifling room, with all the air sucked out, caused sweat to pour from her temple. Once Mother threw shade all over Tetchy, relief came, and she started breathing again.

Leonor and Remedios weren't smiling anymore. They wiped the bitchiness from their faces. They almost looked sad. Even a little resentful. They glared at her. Juliet was still beaming with fear, though her mind was stuck on Juliette. Her dope-sick love. What would Mother say if she knew the truth?

"Regardless," Mother said, "he is my brother's son. A Saramago by marriage. I suppose something must be done."

Their smiles grew. Larger this time. A twinkle in their eyes like a goblin smack ready for the kill. Juliet swore Leonor licked her lips as though she could taste Juliette's blood that hadn't landed in her mouth just yet. The hunger in that girl's eyes she once admired but now despised.

"Mother," Juliet's heart being ripped from her chest.

"No, Juliet." Mother swung her finger like a metronome. "Not this time. After you marry Sebastian Carlito, Leonor will fight. Our ways are our ways. Juliette Marquez pitted against our Leonor."

Leonor beamed. Consoled by a twisted little heart. All the blood in Juliet's body sailed to the floor. The ground beneath fell away. A sourness flooded her mouth. No longer the flavor of juniper. Her stomach brewing like the spa water. Blood pressure skyrocketing. One could view her broken heart from the stars.

"Sebastian isn't my soulmate, I love—"

Mother sprang. The water, more turbulent than before. Purple wisp slid down her face and plunked into the spa water. Steam spewing from her eyes. She was pure fire. Not on point. But the opposite of on point. Brows sharpened in Juliet's direction.

Leonor and Remedios backed away.

"Love, tell me, girl, who is it?"

She silently released "Juliette" from those lips.

The powerful jets drowned out her voice. Leonor and Remedios squinted. Turned their ears and heard only garble. They glanced at each other. Then Juliet. They couldn't decipher the name of Juliet's love.

But Mother had heard. Mother hears everything. "Juliette Marquez?" Her face was dumbstruck. Tone bewildered. Sounding much like Leonor when Devin had blurted Juliette's name. Both their faces equally jacked up.

"What have you done?" Mother stumbling over words. A look of betrayal set in. "You attend River High. She attends Mountain. What gives?" Mother had broken her heart first. Then a daughter, once loyal to a fault, broke Mother.

Juliet—silent. Careful not to mention their seconds of bliss. Falling in love in a matter of seconds during the rager was not a good angle.

"She's my soulmate." Almost on the verge of tears. Mother knew that plea well. Yes, a mother knows the sound of a child's heart dangling over the edge. But could she catch it? Before it splatted into a bloody mess.

What could Mother do? Her only daughter was in love. "There will be no fight for life, nor a wedding." A mother's heart is like a love's heart, stubborn and reckless. Except a mother, most times, will cut off their own head to spare the child.

"I demand you grant me oath!" Leonor smirked at Juliet. *Killing Juliette, might benefit,* she thought. "I'm goanna punch Juliette's clock!"

Mother leaned back. Her words were final. Were law. The matter already tended to in her mind. "Tetchy is my nephew. You have no oath here. Go on and let me be."

Killing Juliette might start a war...let them kill each other... a clever distraction, Leonor thought. She somehow produced tears. Enough to stream down her face. "Tetchy is my oath. My soulmate."

Mother jolted to life again, angrier than before. "Have you all gone mad? Tetchy is married to Frida Carlito! She had his baby. A girl. That baby will be the next Mother in line. I never imagined you were this trashy, Leonor, but you changed my mind today." Mother's voice thundered against the walls and outplayed the jet's boisterous hums.

Leonor wiped her eyes. "I'm pregnant. I demand oath!" Her voice twittery.

Mother's eyes were wide and faraway. She perched in the water like the Loch Ness Monster. "His child?"

For the first time, Juliet felt guilty for falling in love with Juliette. Leonor was her BFF. Juliet tried to console. But Leonor pointed a damning finger. "Don't touch me. You're nothing to me."

Leonor wouldn't even let Remedios console. Remedios felt torn. Loyalty against loyalty. Oath against oath. Remedios decided, *Mother is law.* "We'll care for the child with Mother's blessing, right?"

Mother peered at Leonor and Remedios. "Remedios will help care for the child. No one shall speak of the child's birthright, ever. Or, Leonor, if you're not careful, you might find a challenger who will punch *your* clock."

Mother's words did not comfort a broken heart. Leonor sunk to the floor and fished a lock of hair from her pocket. Remedios and Juliet couldn't trust their eyes. "This is your locket. A promise to right a wrong. Now grant me oath. Juliette will die to pay for her sins."

Juliet gasped a strange combination of sounds. Mother glanced at Juliet, then Leonor.

Travelogue

The *goblin smack* is a ferocious beast at close range. Its razor sharp teeth can slice a person in half. It takes on human form until it's ready to attack. If one should encounter a naked being in the woods, avoid making eye contact. Legend holds a goblin smack hypnotizes with the eyes of a unicorn. One glance renders prey catatonic. People claim the goblin smack devours its victims from the inside.

Salty Squad

"No, Leonor," Mother said. "I won't accept your oath. Not for Tetchy. He's not worth dying over. Everybody knows that. Your oath will start a war. He smashed you without protection like a real shit. He's no longer anyone's concern. Juliette punched his clock. He had it coming, case closed."

"He was going to leave her!" Leonor stomped her feet, trying to muffle that sinister smirk. "He loved me."

Mother's eyes rolled. "Oh, Leonor, don't build an empire on Tetchy's lies. They all say that."

"I was his only love."

Remedios chuckled, then slapped her mouth.

"If you have something to say, then spill it." Leonor sneered.

Remedios sunk eyes to the floor. "My bad."

"Fucking spill it!"

"Bruh, come on," Remedios rested a hand on her hip. "Tetchy chilled with everyone. I mean, *everyone*." Hesitant to say more. Though willing to go further to drive the point. To reason with Leonor's sensible side. If anyone could reach Leonor, it would be Remedios. "I'm sorry, he's fucking shady. He did you dirty like all the others. Can't you see that?"

"Very true, Leonor." Mother raised a finger.

Leonor glared at Mother, then Juliet. Juliet's eyes dialed with sorrow. Remedios spoke to something different. If her eyes could talk, they'd say, *I can't believe you fell for Tetchy's bullshit.*

In return, Leonor glanced at Remedios with a painful face. Almost to say, *I hope you're buying this. You'll dangle from the hook if you don't.*

Remedios turned her head in shame.

Leonor chucked the lock of hair and screamed. Juliet flinched as the scream thundered inside the spa. Leonor pointed at Mother. No one dared point at Mother like that. "If you won't grant me oath, then I'll take it, dead or alive." Then she stormed off.

"Mother, stop her."

Mother didn't seem as nervous as Juliet. Instead, she watched Leonor part. Though something lurked beneath her formidable exterior. Juliet had seen that look once before. When the House of Marquez had delivered a bloody package to the front door. Someone had wrapped father's head inside a decorative box. From that day forward, Juliet would never forget the fear on Mother's face. Juliet would carry that terrifying look to the afterlife.

"Leonor needs time to chill. I mean, big time!" Mother tossed purple wisps onto the cold hammered copper. "She's fucked in the head. We don't go to war over a man. Much less that little prick." Mother balled her fists as though she wanted to strike something.

Remedios gave a worried look. "Damn, she's really salty over Tetchy."

Mother climbed out of the spa, stirring the water like a prehistoric creature rising from the deep. Bubbles covered half her body. Platinum elixir shed all over the stone floor. "Hand me a towel." Mother dried off and dressed in a hurry. "Remedios, invite Mother Marquez for a sit-down. These things are better discussed face-to-face." Mother sat at the vanity made of spider wood while speed-combing her hair. She glared at them through the ancient vanity mirror.

"Marquez's squad won't let me past the gate." Remedios locked eyes, but not for too long. That worried look still clinging to her face.

"Hurry, there's no time to waste." Mother handed Remedios an ancient saint card. The get-out-of-jail-free kind.

"You can't be serious?"

Mother gave a surefire look. "The enemy of my enemy. Now do as you're told."

Remedios did as instructed. Juliet tried to trail after when Mother said, "Don't you dare. I'm not finished with you."

Mother didn't know that Juliet and Juliette had planned to wed today. Mere minutes from now. They would take part in a forbidden ceremony to join two rival families. As long as Sister Claude sanctioned the marriage on a blue jade stone. Then no one could touch them. Not even the Mothers. The only way Juliet and Juliette could escape the grips of Mafia Land was to be out from under the eye of those at the head of the table.

Juliette Marquez had been waiting for Juliet at the Sacred Arché. Sister Claude by her side. Ready to enact the Art of Rubia. Prepared to bind blood with blood. A blood tie that would never break. Even after death. Unless the blood was not true love.

A throng of lilac-birds flew high above the Sacred Arché. Most everyone knew, lilac-birds were a dark sign. But were they? Or were they simply fending off a predator? The only storm in sight was birds. Rattled birds. Twisting and darting like rainbow particles in the afternoon sky.

The day, perfect blue. Suns blinded at twelve, three, six, and nine. Right on the dot. Sixty degrees cooled the skin. They had almost made it, Juliet thought. Mother clung to her hand. She spoke no truer words. "This love is forbidden. You will be a Mother someday. You have your house, and she has hers. That's the order of things. What would Mafia Land be without tradition?" She emphasized the last part. "Mothers cannot share a bed."

"I love her." Her eyes were infallible. Her heart, infallible. Mafia Land had been bleak as hell until now. She would rather die a thousand agonizing deaths without Juliette by her side.

A mother knows a daughter's heart before a daughter does. If the eyes never dart from shame or sin, then it must be true love. But above all, this love is deadly.

Love was not part of Juliet's vocabulary. For one, she grew up thinking love was a twisted game. Fall in love today but dead the next. Mafia Land stole loved ones regularly. She tried her best not to love father or Mother or anyone else. Especially not Sebastian Carlito.

Juliet was a quiet child most of her life. When you're a quiet observer, sometimes you see things for what they are. Some things can never be unseen.

She insulated herself from death through isolation. Then, out of the blue, she brought home Sebastian. Like a stray baba foot. He was a decent boy. More basic than anything. So basic, Mother Saramago said over dinner that evening. Mother knew there would come a time when Juliet brought someone home. Though she had expected more. She didn't know how much more. Just more. Just as anyone would root through clothes on a rack. A person never knows what they're looking for until they stumble upon it. Sebastian wasn't the right anything. He was right-eous as boys go in Mafia Land. For another Juliette. Not *her* Juliet.

Still, Mother was often curious to know what Juliet was missing in life. Juliet spent all those days in her room. She had all the latest gadgets. Access to the finest things in Mafia Land. But an AI doesn't have a heartbeat. No soul to speak. Electricity is never enough to power a soul. A soul who desires love. Connection to something real. Something full of life. Juliet was drowning in a world of endless algo-rithms. Algorithms that sell you stuff. That, fingers crossed, will fill an otherwise empty heart.

When a gentle hand unearths a soundless heart, the heart would rather stop than let go of something so pure. A single beat was all it took. A faint beat among the dark. Lips made of zigzag silk. Breath of juniper. Tongue flavored with whipper sweets. The aftertaste of pepper nips. Because nothing sweet lasts forever in Mafia Land. How does something once sweet turn so bitter? An eye for which another eye lives. Or wildly woven somewhere between two worlds that don't belong. Never could. Never would.

Mother could see Juliet was in love. She never looked that happy with Sebastian. She could not alter her decision. Mother aimed to end the nightmare before it spiraled. Before bodies started piling up. "Juliet, sometimes in a mother's life, she knows she hasn't done her best." Mother watched Juliet's reaction. "I royally fucked up." She scratched the middle of her head. Massaged temples. "For the life of me, I never asked if you were happy. It's not the right word I'm looking for. But it's the best I can do under the circumstance. So, I'll just say it. Are you happy?"

Juliet seemed deflated. She didn't want to destroy Mother twice in one day. "I'm not sure."

Mother inspected Juliet. "I did what was best. But I never considered your happiness." Mother continued grinding her temple as though her thoughts hurt. "I love you very much. I certainly don't say it enough. Now, I'll ask one more time. Are you happy?"

"No." At first, she was ashamed to make eye contact. Not out of being scolded. Rather, she couldn't bear to see Mother suffer.

It's a safe distance to watch heartbreak from a mile away. But eye to eye, that's a different deal altogether. "Tell me, does she make you happy?"

Unbeknownst to Juliet, her face lit up. Eyes glittery as fuck. She sprung to life, as though reviving a dying unicorn. "Yes."

Mother saw something in Juliet she hadn't seen in some time. Pure joy rose from those eyes. "Run to it." Mother's face was elegant as polished stone. The kind that only imperial beauty can pull off. Her silky posture commanded attention. "Love is rare. Catch it before it flutters away like a spotted snow moth."

Mother smiled with a hint of sadness. She knew Juliet's happiness would come at a price. No doubt in her mind. Love would maul Juliet and Juliette to pieces. In Mafia Land, fate dooms love from the start.

"Did you love father? You never cried at his funeral."

"How dare you ask such a thing?"

"Did he love you?"

Mother seemed a little broken. Touched that her daughter would contemplate such things. Juliet imagined no one had ever asked

Mother that question. Nobody had cared enough to ask. "I loved your father because he took one step to my twenty. I suspect there were times he despised me for that. I'll tell you something, Juliet. Love was not your father's strength."

"I'm to wed at Sacred Arché."

"I see." Another worried expression etched on Mother's face. Almost too scared to hear the rest. "When?"

Juliet glanced at her phone to notice several text messages from Juliette. Last one: *HURRY!* The one before: *WHERE R U at Sacred!*

"Now."

Before Mother could get more details, Remedios burst through the spa. "Mother Marquez is on her way. She agreed to a sit-down."

Mother's eyes swam with relief. She handed Juliet a gun, fished from the vanity drawer. Platinum plated with carved stone handles. Boom—loaded. "Take this. I don't trust Leonor. I'll meet you at the Sacred Arché soon. Mother Marquez will join me if all goes well. This marriage must remain a secret."

Panda Bees

MOTHER ALWAYS MADE sure her attire was on point, as in stylish, no exceptions. Especially during sit-downs. Especially when she sat across from another Mother. To be on point signifies a well-ordered house. Not to be, spoke to disorder. Which precipitates chaos. Chaos is favorable under the right circumstance. Ideal during wartime. Otherwise frowned upon during a time of peace.

Today, however, Mother Saramago threw on whatever her hands could grab. A velour track suit. Velour was making a strong comeback. Leisure wear was a fashion of the future. The only thing squads wore.

In reality, she was on the opposite spectrum of on point. Frizzy hair. Tired eyes. Velour glued to her skin. Ridding up everywhere. When she poured herself into that track suit, she toweled off in a hurry. Damp skin clung to every inch of that up-and-coming velour.

* * *

Some Mothers hadn't given a shit about keeping up with appearances for years. Women and girls could wear whatever or as little as they wanted. Makeup was burning somewhere for eternity. Had been for a long time. "Who needs that shit when girls call the shots?" a point guard screamed at a newbie after slapping lipstick out of her hand.

After the Land of Kings went up in smoke, women could do whatever the fuck they wanted. Funny enough, jogging in the dark became popular. Most requested. They weren't jogging to lose weight. Health, maybe. But jogging in the dark and reaching home was the sign of the times.

Men despised the new world. Despised women going to work. Despised these foreign agents who had infiltrated the capital. Who did these women think they were, creating new laws without a man's approval? New ways of doing things caused some serious blowback. But what could they do? For the first time in history, women outnumbered men.

At first, the male population, some females too, tried to destroy a nation led by women. Mother rule proved deadlier than the old. Which annihilated once and for all the ancient world. To make room for something unheard of. Still, new is often nothing more than a tribute to the old.

Others considered Mother Saramago, and those like-minded, retro because the Mothers ruled in the old ways. Out of touch, some squads claimed. Mother Saramago did her best to uphold tradition for the good, but flexible in other ways. This world no longer belonged to the Mothers as it once did. It now belonged to the up-and-coming.

She recognized something the other Mothers did not. The old ways would destroy this generation. Without drastic changes, they would leave nothing for the youth to build on. Juliet's generation was far more efficient at running the schools. Squads mastered the inner workings of a new society better than the Mothers. They knew each student by name and who belonged to which squad. Birthright guaranteed no one a spot on the squad. Whoever wanted to join had to earn it. Without the squads, the Mothers would lose track of who belonged where. Students pledged allegiance to the squads. Squads' allegiance was to the students and the Mothers. Bigger fish to biggest. The order of Mafia Land. Though the order of things had showed cracks.

* * *

Seconds after Juliet raced toward the Sacred Arché, platinum gun in hand, Mother Saramago entered the greenhouse. Ready to deal those bloody saint cards. Do whatever it took to avoid a war.

The greenhouse was more of a solarium, constructed of glass and steel. Plants and flowers as far as the eye could see. Transporting people who sat among the greenhouse to an alien world. A canopy of vegetation devoured glass and reached for the bountiful sky.

Spotted snow moths fluttered about as though locked in a white-out. Throughout the day, the tranquil sounds of widow crickets created a symphonic masterpiece. Even though one bite from a widow cricket could paralyze a child.

Lady jumpers and panda bees whizzed by occasionally, making the rounds. Checking on things. The search for something lush is constant. Something sweet to sink their teeth into. The air smelled of nectar. Buckets and buckets of nectar. Sweet and moist, the air was. Sunlight dappled through the foliage and stippled the floor in disco-light.

Mother Saramago favored this place for mafia matters. Watching nature take its course in a controlled setting. With death dealing along for the ride was a stark reminder that nature, no matter how deadly, is a thing of beauty. Can coexist in times such as these. Often cruel but well balanced with the universe.

Though, deep down, Mother knew a box made of glass and steel was the illusion of control. That tradition, much like an ecosystem, was more fragile than first assessment. Take, for example, the panda bee. If panda bees escaped the box, oh, the damage they'd inflict upon a house made of spider wood. If one should ever escape through the crack of a door, then "pray for us all" should be the next words out of anyone's mouth.

Mother often lay awake at night, wondering if her nightmare would ever come true. Would the panda bee make a lucky break? Or would the panda bee finally wake up and realize it could escape? Was it buying time, waiting for the right moment to strike? If it proved to be the latter, then she'd be in grave danger. Her house of spider wood would fall in seconds because the greenhouse was teeming with hungry panda bees. Then it raised the question: How many more panda bees knew the truth? The only barrier between the house and the greenhouse was a single-pane glass door. The fragility of a well balanced ecosystem.

When Mother Saramago entered the greenhouse. The sight of Mother Marquez struck her. They both wore exacting velour tracksuits. Color and all. Royal indigo. Stripes running down the sleeves and pants. Mother Marquez's hair fixed into a pony. An unusual sight.

Except for today, Mother Marquez always curled her hair to precision. Know thy enemy. Not a stitch of makeup covering that mug. Eyes tired and puffy, like Mother Saramago. No, Mother Marquez wasn't herself today. Neither were playing their parts.

What Mother Saramago wanted to know: Did Mother Marquez already know what she knew? A forbidden love that spiraled into a murder of a made dude. Brought on by Juliet and Juliette. No, she couldn't know about Leonor's deadly threat just yet, Mother Saramago thinks. That only happened minutes ago. Still, surveillance travels light speed these days.

They sat facing each other, stiffly. Scrutinizing one another with calculating eyes. Who would speak first? They had to squash old sins to move forward for the good. For Juliet and Juliette. Details they'd have to sweep under that blunder beetle silk carpet. The details decided everything. Heads shipped in a box were a gruesome jester. That started a war between the two.

Mother Saramago returned the favor and shipped a head or two herself. An eye for an eye. If one is cold enough to say such things. The houses feuded because of bad intel. Intel that was planted. Dissension in the ranks ignited the whole thing.

As they sat across from one another, husbandless, fatherless, they faced another not-so-good-news moment. Would the Mothers revert to old habits and sanction a death note? Single file, one head after another, perhaps?

"It's time to end this feud, wouldn't you agree?" Mother Marquez folded her arms with angry eyes. "I'm to blame for your husband's death. I can't take—"

Mother Marquez shook her head, as though trying to suppress the rage brewing. "I adored my husband, but you, you married because you had no other choice. I had no reason to send you a death note. If I was going to send a death note, I'd send your daughter's head. It's more effective." This bold threat burrowed through her heart like a panda bee. Mother Saramago's eyes beamed, then sharpened.

If the tea spilled, it would be today. They had a long history. They were once BFF, in another life. Before they became mothers and wives. More self-control had to avoid another feud. Less impulse. Cooler heads. Cooler heads save the day. Cooler heads accomplish more, Mother Saramago told herself in the heat of the moment. No, Mother Saramago refused to low-key it. Not this time. "I should have known better."

Mother Marquez was still angry but unfolded her arms. Though, somewhere between, Mother Saramago caught a hint of something. Mother Marquez strangely shifted in her seat. Beyond the steel eyes, sadness peeked through. Mother Saramago saw heartbreak. Mother Saramago's voice was gentler, pleading. "What can I do to set things right?"

Mother Marquez cleared her throat. "I'm not here to discuss old wounds. I came to discuss Juliette and your Juliet and that son of a bitch Tetchy."

Mother Saramago's plumb posture, eased a little. Eager to discuss the Juliet and Juliette love affair. Not so much that son of a bitch Tetchy. "Isn't it fitting an omen such as this would bring us together? We can't catch a break."

They sat, calculating. Words and how to place them just right were more dire than ever before.

"Yes."

They glanced at each other and said, "Fate."

Mother Marquez rubbed her throat. "Damn this cold." Her face puckered as though she had eaten something sour.

"Platinum elixir would clear that right up." Mother Saramago gestured to the attendant standing nearby. "Bring Mother Marquez platinum elixir and a whipper sweets biscuit."

"I can't stand whipper sweets." Mother Marquez waved her hand in protest.

The attendant stopped and peered at them. Mother Saramago shooed him off. Never adjusting the order. Which meant stick to the original order.

"I know you dislike them, but they never failed you before."

Mother Saramago, remembering Mother Marquez's childhood illnesses, touched Mother Marquez.

The attendant served Mother Marquez the elixir and biscuit. She sipped bird like and nibbled the lacey biscuit edge. "My Juliet is in love with your Juliette."

Mother Marquez slammed the elixir onto the table and wiped her mouth. Then snapped off another piece. "Love." She almost laughed. Mentioning love in the same sentence as Juliette and Juliet. "What do they know about love?"

Mother Saramago paused and waited for Mother Marquez to finish chewing. "What I wouldn't give to roll back the numbers to be in love. Childish love at that."

"They're fortunate. These are different times." Mother Marquez was still munching. "What we do," she motioned her finger back and forth, biscuit in hand, "afford them the luxury to love." Mother Marquez sat a little taller. "What about Tetchy? Reparations are in order. Fight for life is tradition."

Mother Saramago's eyes stayed true and focused. "Not this time. Tetchy had it coming. Juliette punched his clock, rightfully so. A jealous lover surely would have."

"It was an accident."

Mother Saramago carefully set the elixir on the armrest. "Oh." Surprise filled her. "Leonor said nothing to that degree. This changes things."

"What things?"

Mother Saramago's face grew squinty. "Well, that's why I

requested a sit-down. Tetchy smashed Leonor. Now she's pregnant and vengeful. She wants Juliette's—"

Mother Marquez rolled her eyes. "Your nephew is a booster. He'll smash anything with a hole. I wouldn't put it past him to smash a pecker."

"How can I argue?" Mother Saramago said. "I tried to end the feud, but Leonor refuses to obey."

"You wouldn't."

"I refused her oath."

Mother Marquez's face showed signs of relief. Her eyes rolled as though she ate something scrumptious. "What about Frida Carlito?"

What Mother Saramago had failed to mention, or omitted, was that she had given Leonor the green light to settle oath. A fight to the death involving none other than Juliette Marquez. She changed her mind after discovering Juliet was in love with Juliette.

"Leonor is bloodthirsty. Her loyalty hasn't gone unnoticed among the squads." Mother Saramago gently eased the conversation. Choosing her words. Trying to keep a straight face. "I'm not so sure of her intentions. I've never seen her this way before. I believe she loved Tetchy, despite the absurdity of it. But you know what childish love can do."

"How could she crush on that little son of a bitch?" She wore a disgusted expression, as though she'd bitten her tongue.

Mother Saramago smirked. She must remain neutral at all costs. One mustn't delight too much in the death of a family member. "I'm just as confused."

"My sources tell me Frida Carlito isn't interested in challenging Tetchy's murderer."

"Is that a fact?" Mother Saramago's eyebrow rose.

Mother Marquez rubbed her palms together to show she had squashed the ordeal.

"We can't be sure of anything. Our daughters might be in danger."

"Will you fight for my Juliette?"

Mother Saramago waited for the perfect moment. It's all in the eyes. Too fast spells desperation. Too slow spells foe. "Without question." Mother Saramago drank the elixir to ease the tension. It had sat iced on the stone table the whole time. "Will you do the same?"

Before Mother Marquez could answer, the gate attendant came rushing into the greenhouse. She was panting, eyes dilated to hell. Battle face applied. "Mother Saramago." The gate attendant barreled over, sucking up air. "It's Juliet."

Mother Marquez shot up, fists clenched, eyes wide. "My Juliette?"

Platinum & Pepper Nips

Contrary to popular medical science, oxygen deprivation kills the brain last. This organ cashes chips several minutes after the heart stops. Dr. Lister worked at Whitehead Academy. Where he stumbled upon a strange discovery. Brain-cell activity still registered three days after death. Dr. Lister concluded the human brain sends sensory information to a carcass already recorded in the Good Book. Sound comforts the mind long after the clock stops. Once the heart surrenders to one last pump and the blood spoils. The sensors that once delighted now haunt.

Would one know when Death collected a toll? Could one still hear a trolley whiz by on the street? The sound of a bicycle bell? An ice cream truck twinkling its faint music? Is it platinum flavored or pepper nips? One can never tell which. Once the clock has been punched.

Dr. Lister wrote these notes right before *his* clock got punched. These haunting questions remained a mystery for years. What can the dead tell the living? Until today.

* * *

Juliet raced to Sacred Arché, where Juliette Marquez waited for her. She wore a mini with a deep shade of indigo. A color reserved for Mothers. In this time and in ancient, proper attire for the Art of Rubia was tradition. She had no time to fix her hair. To wear the right shoes. Only enough time to slip on the dress and run out the door. The day wouldn't allow much more than that. No matter how dry the elbows were. Dry elbows marked the season. Would Juliette care if Juliet's elbows were prickly as hell?

In Mafia Land, women didn't wear white at a wedding. They forbade it. Unless one was trying to summon a goddess from the Land of Kings. The color a woman wore on her wedding day didn't determine her value. Rather, the woman she was every day after the long war.

Juliet came upon the Sacred Arché while Juliette Marquez lied on the blue jade stone that centered it. Her eyes were closed. She was sleeping at a time like this. Or at least that's what Juliet thought. Wearing an indigo mini too. A deeper shade than Juliet. Almost black under certain light. The Art of Rubia scribbled on her body. Down her arms and legs. Let's not forget the hands and feet. Hair braided with precision. Juniper dust sprinkled wherever the eye landed. Burnt offerings and whipper sweets wafted from her. All four suns beating down. A gentle breeze swept pebbles along the eroded stone on which she lay.

Juliet knelt beside her and whispered in her ear, "I love you."

Saying *I love you* was cringe. Few used that phrase anymore. It reminded them of the Land of Kings. But appropriate for the Art of Rubia.

Seconds tolled. Juliet stared at Juliette, waiting for her to wake. For those eyes to flutter to life. A leg to stir. Fingers to twitch. Her chest to pop and sink. One stroke. Two strokes. Then nothing. Body still. Juliette was a castaway.

She nudged Juliette hard. "Hey, this isn't funny anymore."

Juliette didn't stir. Didn't spring to life. Juliet panicked. Her heart fluttering fast. Enough to fuel two hearts. Two souls stroking out. She cast eyes everywhere, searching for Sister Claude. Where was Sister Claude? Juliet shook her. "Juliette!" Her voice shattered. "Juliette!"

Those loving tears pouring everywhere could not revive. "Juliette!" She would not wake to the voice of love. Would not stir. Her body, heavy. Limbs of steel. Juliet lifted her hands to hold, to cling. They were still warm. Velvety as life.

Juliet kept saying, "Juliette." As though the sound of her voice could cure death. Chills climbed into her soul. Those tingles rooted in the heart went somewhere. Tingles she had never felt before. Tingles that had once belonged to love but now wore death. Death were the new tingles.

Juliet went silent. Tears still going. Her face was serious now. She swore Juliette had moved a second ago. But was she seeing things? She skimmed every inch of Juliette's body, hoping she had made a mistake. That her eyes had fluttered. She waited for them to flutter again. Open would be best.

Nothing happened. It was purely an optical illusion. Or psychosis. Or dreaming. Or all the above. "No!" The heartbreaking wail rose. A wail that speaks of love lost. Love that could never be. Love that never was. Bringing a quick end to her soulmate.

"It's not supposed to go like this." She mopped her face. Frustrated by her emotions. She kissed Juliette, passionate and gentle, as though she might break her. Her nose was all gooey. Her lips were still warm and silky. How could she still taste the juniper and whipper sweets?

She sat there for a minute, staring off into the distance. Then two. Then three. On the third, something came to her. What would Mafia Land be like without Juliette? Could she live without Juliette? Maybe a second longer than this, perhaps. Nanosecond is best.

She somehow made it past three and nine quarters without Juliette. Though most of those minutes and seconds had carried over because of hope. That Juliette would spring to life. Now she was facing the fallout. Mothers teach love. Its complexities. Inner workings. How the system runs. How it heals in time if one should be so lucky. That way, when the time comes, children know how to deal with the hardest part—a broken heart.

Love made the day eternal. In the darkest way possible. Love lived on the outskirt of death. One can never be too sure about these matters. Death bares no tongue.

She sat there squeezing Juliette's hand. Tears for days. Nothing could fill the endless well of tears. Her hand gripped the gun. The weight of cold-plated platinum. A key which could open a door to the ever after.

She heard a widow cricket snare emitting from Juliette's heart. But she wouldn't trust her ears. One snare, two snare, three snare. Faster and faster. Now running toward liftoff. Soaring through the clouds, squeezing past the stars, traveling elsewhere. A snare beating somewhere in the deep darkness, surrounded by nothing. Faint snare. There snare. Right over there. In the corner. Hurry, Juliet, you might just miss it.

In reality, when people come to quick conclusions, even in death, nothing is what it seems. Not always. Not in Juliette's case. The word of the day is *catalepsy*. Pronounced as written. Free of gimmicks. No silent vowels to fool with, just catalepsy.

Juliet's initial kiss, however short, overshadowed Juliette Marquez's cataleptic condition. Juliet didn't know that Juliette would lose consciousness at all the wrong times. A cataleptic episode that resembles death in a very scary way. A weak pulse and shallow breaths made it seem like Juliette was dead. It even deceived the brightest doctors in the land.

Her snare heartbeat teetering between life and death was often the case. Razor thin sometimes does life hang in the balance. Sleeping next to the dead, are we? Checking out at midnight before gray dust is served. A little gray death, anyone?

Juliette Marquez was very much alive. Only unconscious. Waiting for true love to revive. To kiss her. Maybe for all eternity. Well, Mafia Land eternity anyway.

* * *

Sometimes, time cannot heal the scars of the past. Amazon delivered her father's head when Juliet walked past the front door at that precise moment. Opening an Amazon package is like opening a birthday gift. People open packages even if they aren't addressed to them. Why does everyone want to peek inside the box? What's in there, anyway? Human nature, I suppose.

The air crackled with excitement. A luxurious package such as this must be hiding delicacies. She ripped open the box and peeked inside. The head placement was off a tad. Not the effect one wants when sending a message. Tipped over during shipment, most likely. The back of his head was the first thing she saw. Dark, fuzzy hair. Matted and mashed to one side. The smell of fermentation traveled to her nose.

It took a few moments riffling through the box to reveal the most haunting treasure. It looked like a mannequin head. It didn't look real. Not to her. A movie prop. A cruel joke. Eyes cashed toward the heavens. Mouth agape. Father was blowing a silent raspberry. *Raspberry*, she thought. *Raspberry*.

The smelly slime and goo horrified. Not a drop of blood in sight. Everything glittered strangely. Wrapped in gold tissue paper. Where does one buy gold tissue paper? Special order is the answer. His head cauterized and pickled.

She screamed a thunderous cry, as any child would. But she never opened her mouth. She did it inside. Standing there, clinging to the box, speechless. She didn't want to let him go. If she set down the box, it raised the question: Did Juliet have the temperament to carry out motherly duties when the time came?

In a strange turn of events. She went back to relive old wounds. She refused to let Juliette go, like father's box. The heart wants what the heart cannot have. She decided a good life had nothing to do with age. Pointless even. Without the one you loved riding shotgun.

She would not cruise through life without love one second longer. Heavy barrel in hand, she pointed the gun at her temple. "I love you."

She peered at Juliette one last time and squeezed. Spotted snow moths scattered like unicorns. A body doesn't drop right away, as one would surmise. She lingered there for a moment. The gunshot buzzing in her ears like a swarm of panda bees.

Juliet saw a beating sun, not four. Then white. Then nothing. Blackness collected her. Her body, not her own anymore, compressed and hit the stone. She lie next to her love. The flesh crumpled, imperfectly. The buzzing wore off. Or maybe she had grown comfortable with the buzz. She heard a lilac-breasted whistle in the distance. Calling to her. She no longer tasted juniper or whipper sweets. Those flavors had long evaporated. Metal mouth converted to pepper nips. Hot and angry. Her mouth was on fire. Now, her mouth was platinum and pepper nips.

Then raspberries. She smelled raspberries for some odd reason. It seemed Dr. Lister was on to something.

Travelogue

The *Art of Rubia* is a forbidden practice from a phantom tribe that lived in the most uninhabitable places on the planet. The ritual has taken many forms throughout the centuries. But one consensus remains. Forbidden love awakens Rubia. Star-crossed lovers must paint their bodies with the plant of Rubia, inscribed in the ancient symbols, to ward off Rubia's deadly wrath. Death to people who do not complete the ritual.

Leonor, Knock Three Times

When Leonor left the House of Saramago, Uncle Stigmata's plan unraveled just a tad. She unraveled. Her sanity was so-so. Which is a one way ticket to the afterlife for a trained assassin. "Never get personal," Uncle Stigmata would say after tasering her with a blabber hoof prod. She had thought of telling Frida Carlito about the affair. About Tetchy being a little booster who somehow turned into a Romeo before her eyes.

Leonor was no ordinary assassin. She was gifted. One of the best that had ever graced the land. According to Uncle Stigmata. He should know, since Uncle Stigmata had trained them all. To the moment the Land of Kings fell.

She fantasized about all the creative ways a person can die. Juliette's murder. Both Juliets. If she didn't get her way. Pushing someone off a tall building was amateur night. Assassins love to hear the splat. Last breath. The carnage one makes on impact. It's not intimate enough to hear an ear-splitting scream on the way down. With the lights on full blast. Curtains ripped open to the world while sitting in front of a mirror inspecting the face. The O face. Not that O face. But a face that yawns because killing no longer thrills. Sick mind. Sick games. Not sick like cool, rather, sick like—*Oh, no, how could you, Leonor?*

And what about Remedios? Leonor had never considered Juliet her BFF. Juliet was BFF with her. Not the other way around. Remedios was her BFF. *But was she?* Leonor considered this question. She was living a double life. Why did she care anyway? Remedios didn't have her back. Never did. Never BFFs from the jump.

It seemed their little squad wasn't close from the get-go. Juliet didn't know that Leonor despised her. And Leonor didn't know that Remedios knew about the affair. Tetchy and Leonor had kept Juliet in the dark too. They were not 4lifers. Never were. It seemed everyone in the squad was living a double life.

* * *

On a sweaty day in August, Remedios stumbled in on Leonor topping Tetchy. Leonor's back was facing the door. With eyes clenched, Tetchy moaned like a cheetah mule. What an eye scrubber that was. Keep quiet. Shut your mouth. Don't leave the door cracked, if you please. The take-away was this: the sound of a cheetah mule braying and three scars on Leonor's back. They seemed to be the instrumental workings of torture. Torture that the State Department passes out like whipper sweets.

The Saramago squad made the championship. Many games and many showers during the season. The only person who never took a shower was Leonor. She played tough. In reality, the squad knew something wasn't right. Sometimes she'd say, "I don't want you bitches snacking on a real bod." Some girls stared. Some laughed. But that was Leonor.

Leonor played as though she had the bod. But she was no Heather. Juliet Saramago was a Heather. *What does it matter anyway*, Remedios thought. *Squad is squad. No one is above the other.*

After walking in on Tetchy and Leonor, it finally made sense why Leonor had shied away from the locker room. The squad was all up in whispers about Leonor and shower time.

It mattered little to Leonor about the rumors. She shrugged it off when a girl in the locker room whispered, "How could Leonor not smell that nasty coming off her?"

No one on the squad had the guts to tell it to her face. Second-in-command syndrome, perhaps. Or fear. Fear was a greater possibility. Leonor could kill on a dime for reasons only known to Leonor.

Leonor was not a pick-me-girl personality type. But now that she thought of it, Leonor never exposed her back. Leonor was on the sneaky link with Tetchy. If she could hide this from the squad. Then what else was she hiding? That's when Remedios realized something was wrong. Remedios should have seen the red flags. Still, she couldn't shake the biggest question: why Tetchy, of all people?

Remedios's mother had once told her love and broken people attract. Broken people fall for the wrong ones and call it love. That kind of love can be a drug. Leonor never trusted the squad enough to reveal her scars. Even though she had pledged 4life. For whatever reason, she trusted Tetchy enough to strip down, scars and all. Who's the asshole? The squad or Leonor, she wondered.

Maybe Leonor thought the squad would get judgy. Or Tetchy excelled at manipulating girls. It never occurred to Remedios that maybe Leonor had manipulated Tetchy. Not like that was hard to do.

* * *

Leonor bypassed the House of Carlito altogether. Instead, she visited the Whitehead Academy. Everyone knew in Mafia Land the best advice came from Whitehead. More to the point, Salvador, the accountant at Whitehead.

One could spin this situation a million ways. Enough to get everyone killed. And ruin Uncle Stigmata's plan. Should she list the aid of Frida Carlito? Or should she do everyone a favor and just kill Juliette Marquez? Maybe even punch Juliet Saramago's clock for safe measure. That daring decision would be determined at a later time. She hoped Salvador could provide more clarity to this dilemma.

They settled Whitehead Academy for Gifted Adolescents outside the region of Mafia Land. Considered a neutral turf. Or better, neutral ground. A good place to start when needed sound advice. This is Mafia Land. One could use a hint of advice on the daily. Art of war was a nasty business. What better place to get advice than from the Masters of War?

In the crystal-lined entryway, a child of ten sat behind the reception desk. Smug little thing. Humming a bizarre tune. Grim notes floating upward and parting somewhere out into the yonder. Hair parted with precision and slicked to one side. Florescent spectacles aimed at a digital pad. "You don't have an appointment." A proper voice sparked to life. Perfect annunciation. Clear resonance. Bearing the essence of finishing school. The boy was still reading. Still humming. No eye contact.

Leonor's eyes cast dead center. A strange look appeared on her face. Was she being punked? "How do you know?" She wore an expression as though she wanted to spring over the counter and spank his little ass.

He stopped reading. Hum zipped tight. "Because." He brandished the digital tablet. The glow of the blue light sparkled in her eyes. "It's two minutes, past three." He pointed at a vacant slot on the digital schedule. "There's no appointment set for three. It doesn't matter because you'd be late. So, dip." When he said *dip*, he nearly screamed the word. His voice bounced off the crystal walls to a clamorous stir.

"Dip," Lenore muttered. Her eyes narrowed. Face white hot. "Listen, you little shit," Particles of spit flew everywhere. "I'm here to see Salvador."

The boy removed his glasses. Stunned, Leonor had mentioned Salvador's name. "Whose house?"

"The House of Saramago," she said. Leonor had lied. She no longer had a squad. No longer a Saramago. Skirting the idea of pledging allegiance to the House of Carlito. Or whoever would grant her oath. If Frida Carlito decided not seek revenge.

The boy dashed off a few words on the tablet and hit send. A faint whooshing sound pinged. He waited. The tablet chimed. He seemed shocked by what he read. His voice was less smug. "The accountant will see you." He pointed toward the crystal elevators. "Sixth floor."

"I know how to get there."

A little girl, nose stuck in a digital tablet, rode the elevator up. Humming that same eerie tune. Except her tone made the whole thing sound more pleasant. Upbeat even. Not so doomsday. Leonor inspected her. She never made small talk. Not usually. Except in elevators. Uncomfortable silence and tight spaces made her nerves crawl. "What are you reading?"

The little girl didn't stop reading. Nor look up. Though the hum went away. She said, using an adorable voice, *Day Follows Night.*

She did a double take. "Serious?"

The little girl kept reading. "Yep." Cutesy, cutesy, she was all the way to Whitehead hell.

But how cutesy could she be? The child was wearing the House of Carlito coat of arms on her sleeve. A child of Carlito was more likely to slit a throat in plain daylight. *Maybe a two-headed sphinx playing with a baba foot before the kill looks adorable from a distance? But only from a distance.*

As she rode the elevator, Leonor wondered, *Can a child absorb this novel? Which raises the question: what was the boy reading?*

Nothing stays the same. The Whitehead vibe had transformed. Where the hell did all these kids come from? The little girl exited on the fifth floor. When she walked past Leonor, she leaked fumes. Toxic and potent. Something rubbed off by a doll or stuffed animal. Raspberries. She smelled of fake raspberries.

When Leonor entered the accountant's office, he was waiting for her. Shelved digital tablets towered behind. An entire wall dedicated to them. Not a single title, she knew. Each color coded and legal.

Salvador placed his arms on the desk and sat with proper posture. Unlike the children, he didn't have his nose buried in a digital tablet. His eyes were sleepy, as though unamused. Annoyed best says it. His mannerisms exuded snobbery. A rare snobbery that only an expensive education could inflate. Though his milky left eye gave her the creeps.

Despite some blue rising to the top. His skin was the texture of gold tissue paper. "What is it now, Leonor? Dug another hole, did we?"

She didn't respond. She took a seat and devoured him with those murderous eyes. Salvador twirled his boney hands. "My time is valuable. Best speed things along."

"Juliette Marquez punched Tetchy's clock." Her expression pained. On the verge of tears.

Salvador smiled with radiant eyes. He opened his palm as though Leonor were supposed to place something in it. "And?"

Leonor grinned whenever she told a lie. "I'm pregnant."

Salvador bounced to his feet and clasped his forehead. "You little dummy. What have you done?" He shook his head. "Tetchy, of all people."

"I'm here for counsel, not judgment."

"Your timing couldn't be deadlier, I'm afraid." He glared at her. "Wipe that smirk off your face."

Leonor flung the chair out from underneath and pointed. "You owe me."

He gasped. Hand clutching his heart. "You have some nerve."

"You owe Addy." She stepped closer. Almost climbing over the desk to choke him out. "Which means you owe me."

Adelaide, a.k.a., Addy. Leonor's older sister by five years was once the brightest student at Whitehead.

* * *

The Octo-tree was a popular hangout during lunch. Students would eat underneath its pink canopy. On a rainy Monday. Years ago. At eleven forty-five on the dot. Addy climbed the tree and hung herself from the highest limb. One that stretched past the canopy. An arm reaching out to the portals of four suns.

Salvador discovered her body swaying in the wind. Salvador never ate lunch in the courtyard. Though he enjoyed watching lilac-birds at play. Their endless song resonated against the backdrop of a drizzle.

They only sang in the rain. He discovered Addy's body first. What terrible luck.

Ten minutes before ending her life, she had sat in the back of the classroom. Observing those around. Seen by everyone but not heard. Seeing someone but not hearing them makes them practically invisible. She was invisible. *Would they care? Would he care?* Little Miss Seen And Not Heard.

Try as he may, he couldn't get her down quick enough before the students piled into the courtyard for lunch. He thought, *Why would students eat out here on a day like this?*

At first, he lifted her drenched body. But dead weight from that height weighs more than a truckload of gold. The rope was so slick, he couldn't get a handle on it fast enough. He still thought about her to this day. How a student could weigh so much.

Someone found a note in her locker after they cut her down. She had died of a broken heart. Not by a student. But by an instructor. Not just any instructor, Tetchy's father, Fernando Saramago.

Fernando, shaken by the event, denied ever having had a romantic relationship. Or any student. Rumors grow legs, as they often did in Mafia Land. The authorities investigated the matter. Neither confirmed nor denied the rumors. Nor cleared his name.

Nine days later, Fernando Saramago put a bullet through his eye. He didn't die right away from the gunshot wound. He lived two years longer. Two very long years. Not able to feed himself. Bathe. Use the bathroom. Wheelchair bound. Not able to speak. A bullet did not claim his life, a clogged artery did. That's how the world solves its mysteries these days.

Ten days later. One tragic event after the other. They didn't consider the Octo-tree a wonder any longer. The Octo-tree wasn't a tree anymore. Instead, they saw a coffin. They saw Addy hanging from its arms. Head turned down. Eyes cast somewhere on the floor.

They gathered tools. Whatever they could get their hands on. Whatever was in eyeshot to satisfy a mob's taste for revenge. Whatever struck the eye first is what they used to beat the tree to nothing. For doing nothing. It takes more than a few trinkets and an hour's worth of sweat to tear down a thousand years rooted in the soil. No matter how many bodies you throw at it. On the eleventh day, a demolition crew took care of the rest. Class dismissed.

They refused to memorialize that spot. Where the tree once lived. Happiness no longer lived there. They refused to speak its name or hers. Whitehead, the collective, knew names have power. And calling out its name only provided more fuel. Evil, like misery, loves company and spreads across the land.

* * *

Leonor cooled down and sat. Never taking her eyes off Salvador, as though trapped in a cage with a goblin smack. He calmy leaned his elbows on the desk. Fingers brushed to form a triangle. "How would you like me to proceed?" He gave her a disgusted look. "I'll caution you—the House of Carlito is a formidable family. The most powerful dynasty in the land. Might as well call them the House of Assassins."

Leonor rolled her eyes. "Does it look like I'm scared? Everybody knows they're fire."

Salvador cackled with a look of disbelief. "Fire? As in lit?" He paused and waited for her reaction. "No, I'd hardly describe the House of Carlito as lit. They're far from lit."

"Then do your job. Tell me what to do."

He sat there thinking, mulling things over. Eyes searching. Now, he looked scared. Leonor couldn't decide whether he feared for her or himself. "We're a neutral party. We take no sides, remember?"

"When did Whitehead educate the House of Carlito? Doesn't seem neutral to me."

He didn't miss a beat. "Whitehead welcomes greatness. Greatness comes from anywhere. You know this."

She kept a keen eye on him. Then he stared. Embroiled in a stare down. "You'd wage war on two of the most powerful dynasties? You?"

Leonor didn't blink. Her facial expression fixed. Determined to seek blood. Salvador twirled his boney hand. Twirl the hand. Twirl the hand. "You can trade birthright for oath, I suppose."

"I have no birthright."

Salvador rolled his eyes and pointed at her belly. "Tetchy's child has birthrights, regardless of infidelity. Tetchy boosted the wrong girl this time." He almost amused himself. "Contractually, your womb belongs to the Carlitos now. You bear a claim against the House. If," he held his index finger to the sky, "the child is a girl. She could be the next Mother. You know as well as I, the Mothers are all about tradition."

Leonor was a little too good at playing the game. She was a natural-born hunter. Without Salvador, she couldn't have pieced everything together. Not quick enough. She was remarkably smart. But suffered from blood lust. In Mafia Land, one must keep their eye on the ball and all the players on the board, legally speaking.

As she sat across from Salvador, a light grew within. Bright eyed. Brows hiked to the ceiling. An epiphany scribbled on her face. The ah-ha moment where everything comes into focus. "Can I trade a birthright for oath?"

Salvador had no poker face. Often, his face spoke faster than his tongue. When Leonor focused on the oath over birthright. Salvador's expression was priceless. As though someone had knocked an ice cream cone from his hand. Double scoop even. "Someone has done this once before. Do you want to know how that ended?" His voice was low, with reminiscent qualities.

"Does it matter?"

"The devil may care," he mumbled.

She flailed her arms.

He peered at her. Raised his tone louder than necessary. "The devil may care!"

Leonor made a face, as though she had eaten something nasty.

"Leonor, you're bright, but you can't even tie your shoes the right way."

"I tie my shoes!"

He wagged his finger and chuckled. "That's not literal. You're not getting it. Let me tell you something. Some time ago, we had a gifted student. There was only one problem. Simple things seemed to stump her. The girl could do calculus inside her head but couldn't tie her shoes. Everyday life fowled her up. Those tiny details are more important than you think. She was useless in the outside world." He paused. Eyes thinking.

"Well?"

Salvador filched, as though yanked from a daydream.

Leonor's eyes were razor. "Tell me what happened."

Salvador cleared his throat. "She fell down a manhole and cracked her head. Died of a brain hemorrhage, so the doctor said."

"She probably didn't see it coming. Nose stuck in a digital tablet or something."

Salvador shook his head. "I'm afraid that wasn't the issue. When they rescued her, she was still alive. Sharper than ever. When they asked how the accident occurred, she said…get this." Salvador appeared as though he wanted to nudge Leonor with his elbow. But she was sitting too far away. "'I thought it was safe to walk over the manhole because there weren't any orange cones.' Can you believe that?" He's smiling, all dumbstruck over himself. "Orange cones signify danger. No cones, no danger. Leonor, invisible cones surround you. Are you going to fall down a manhole and crack your head? Do you really need someone to tell you danger lurks ahead, or can you read the signs?"

Leonor sat there unfazed, cold even. More determined than ever while vengeance swam in those veins. Wearing a smug face. Smug as the boy down at reception.

"Do you even desire a crown?"

Leonor's eyes darted, spilling facts along the way as they climbed toward the ceiling.

"I suppose you're right. A crown can't vie with revenge." He knocked his fist on the desk three times. "Godspeed, Leonor. Godspeed."

Travelogue

A millennium before the academy's construction, someone mysteriously planted the *Octo-tree*. It is unparalleled. The architect who built Whitehead fell in love with its untamed limbs and foliage. A place where fairies dwell, the architect often said. She built the academy around the tree, brick by brick. She was careful not to destroy the root system during the extraordinary build.

The *blabber hoof* is a two-legged animal that rolls around in the mud most of the day and stinks to the highest order. Its full-time job comprises grazing in lush pastures and supplying the world with blabber hoof milk. Which lowers blood pressure. Equalizes blood-sugar levels. But tastes like purple wisp clippings and spoiled mud and excrement.

Smash Königsmarck

In the House of Carlito, only Mother is king. A queen maker. When Frida heard the news of Tetchy's death, she cared little. Said little. Went about her life as though nothing had happened. The baby girl by her side was more important. For the first time in quite a while, she played on the floor with little Mia. Rolled around on the floor, making silly faces. Little Mia, Tetchy's daughter, would be the next Mother in line.

Hearing the news of Tetchy's death somehow relieved her. Freed her from years of strife. Frida no longer needed to pretend. No blinders required to get on with life. Rumors and surveillance footage of Tetchy's boosting ways were behind her now. Not only was Tetchy an unfaithful love, but he was also an absent father. *Tetchy resents being a father*, she thinks. Or resented. Past tense. *How is that a child's fault?*

Mother Carlito rushed into the room, alarmed. "Have you heard?" Mother peered down at Frida lying on the floor with little Mia.

Frida smiled at Mia. "No, Mother, I haven't. And I don't care." She nuzzled Mia's nose and used a baby's voice. "Right? We don't care." Mia smiled with wandering eyes.

Mother sat next to Frida on the blunder beetle silk carpet. "Two more girls in the last hour have challenged birthright." Mother flicked two fingers in the air. "They're pregnant with Tetchy's baby. That booster."

Frida, still playing with little Mia, used that baby voice again. "We don't care, do we?"

Mother motioned to the attendant. "Take the child for a stroll. The suns will do her some good."

The attendant nodded and scooped little Mia from the floor. "Mother?"

Mother grabbed Frida by the arm. "This is very serious. There are five girls challenging birthright. Who knows how many more are out there? They can challenge Mia's right to be Mother."

"I'll be Mother first. It won't matter after that."

Mother shook Frida. "Did you know?"

"I'm not stupid."

Mother's eyes popped. Panic had given way to disappointment. "How long?"

Frida didn't answer. Her expression stuck in thinking mode.

"How long?"

"After Mia was born. Well, maybe during the pregnancy. We weren't having sex."

"So, what does that have to do with anything? A boy can take care of himself."

"Technically, he did."

"That's not what I meant, and you know it. What kind of boy boosts girls on the side while his pregnant wife is at home?"

"Boys too."

"Boys?" Mother's voice was high-pitched. "I'd rather he smash boys than girls. Boys can't get pregnant." *But could they*, she wondered after making that statement. *Can't* is like *never*. Use those words sparingly. Under the rarest of occasions. Mother glared at Frida for confirmation if boys could get pregnant. *Who knows these days*, she often said.

Frida's lips quivered. Waterworks rose. "I confronted him the first time I found out."

Mother listened with razor eyes. Her hands rotating. Head bobbing. "What did the boy say?"

"He said, he said," Frida edged toward a crying spell, "I'm not porn material."

Mother can't believe her ears. "Porn material?" She said *porn material* as though she couldn't hardly believe those words were escaping. "Porn material? He really said that to you? These boys, always thinking with their little, tiny pricks." Mother pantomimed an imaginary penis in her hand. "They can't even wipe their ass."

"Right," Frida said, voice quivering. "He always left skid marks in his underwear. It's gross."

Mother tried not to laugh, as serious as the situation was. Heartbroken as Frida was. Yet laughed instead. Frida looked horrified as the tears splashed on the blunder beetle silk carpet. Mother's inappropriate laughter made the atmosphere humorous. Then Frida caved. They both erupted in laughter.

"I knew that boy was no good." Mother wore a more sympathetic face. "I knew you loved him. That boy had unicorns shining out of his ass in your eyes. I wanted you to be happy. Someone in this family deserves happiness."

Don't fret. Mafia Land is big. But also the size of a quark. Love is like water. It finds a way inside. Someone fell hard for Frida, despite Tetchy's unreasonable claim.

An attendant named Königsmarck thought Frida was the universe. He gave things a go. And, boy, did they go. A little too well. Everywhere it could. In the bedroom. The ballroom. After dismissing the cooks, they rushed into the kitchen, laughing, kissing, and grabbing. Getting naked. It continued on and on. Outside in the maze of shrubs. In Mother's sacred room. The library. Passion is like a baby. It cries at inconvenient times. It wakes people up during the night. Interrupts breakfast. Or out on a Sunday stroll.

The kitchen staff knew. All the attendants were aware. The only person who didn't know of the love affair was Mother. Two days ago, Mother had interrupted their smash session. Königsmarck saw Mother riffling through papers in the sacred room. He saw all this from behind a velvety sofa. Their favorite spot. The sofa faced a large window that gave a view of the meadow out back. It was a thing for some time.

Mother never caught them in the act. Still, the fear of getting caught did not detour them. It seemed to charge the air. Fuel their passion. Sometimes the guilt of doing something naughty feels right. Even though it shouldn't.

They carried on as usual. Once, Mother had slammed the door behind her. Then, an hour later, tidied up the place. Arranging the sofa pillows. Fixing hair and clothes. Fooling the eye into thinking they had not been rolling around on that expensive blunder beetle silk carpet.

Pheromones electrify oxygen molecules. Then travel the body. The senses. Passion leaves a lasting imprint. It's difficult to gloss over the aftermath of smashing. It's a hard to fool the eye.

Frida and Mother were still laughing when Königsmarck interrupted them. "Mother Carlito."

Mother looked up, the joy draining from her face. "What is it now?" Mother gave Frida a funny look.

When Mother turned her head, Königsmarck mouthed "I love you" to Frida. Frida smiled. Her face glowed when he said it. Frida struggled to conceal her infatuation. Her eyes devoured every inch of him.

Mother had seen that same look on Frida before. The look of a diseased heart. Tetchy love. She glanced at Königsmarck and studied him. But he was faster than Mother. And put on a business-as-usual face seconds before Mother turned her head back around.

He hides his love for Frida well. Mother thinks. Königsmarck. Smart. Athletic. Face card valid. Mia adores him. A better boy than Tetchy.

"Mother, Leonor Saramago requests a sit-down." His voice beamed with mad respect for Mother. One must consider the facts when assessing Frida and Königsmarck's relationship. Mother softened her tone. "I've seen enough girls today. I can't take more bad news."

Königsmarck stood there with a troubling expression. "She stabbed a guard."

Mother rose from the floor. "Has she gone mad?" Her eyes sizzle with disbelief. "Did she kill them?"

"No." He kept staring at Frida. He couldn't stop looking at her. Eyes darting from Frida to Mother, Mother to Frida. "The medic has stabilized the guard. She will live."

"Is that girl smoking gray dust?" Mother's voice rose, confused. She stood there for a moment, thinking about the best course. "Is she?"

"No, she's in custody now. It took a minute."

"Good." Mother's voice was uncertain. Her eyes bewildered. "I will grant Leonor a sit-down."

Frida stood. "I'll go too, Mother."

Königsmarck interjected. "It's not safe."

"Not safe?" Mother peered at him as though she could read whatever was going on in his brain. "I'll settle Leonor. Spring cleaning is long overdue. Bring her to the library."

A peculiar lounge occupied a section of the library. Two oversized sofas faced off. Separated by a massive gold coffee table. Mother and Frida sat on one side, and Leonor on the other. Surrounded by guards and handcuffed. Her hands resting in her lap in a cutesy way.

Leonor wore the same look Frida had: Tetchy love. Mother recognized that look. "How far along are you?" Mother said. "By the looks of it, not far at all."

Leonor seemed surprised. Mother Carlito knew the tale without saying a word. "I demand oath against Juliette Marquez."

Mother laughed, flapped her hand. "Who are you to demand anything? Only Mother Saramago can grant you oath. That is tradition. You belong to her house."

"Mother Saramago granted me oath. I just need your blessing."

Mother Carlito sniffed out the lie. She knew Leonor was playing a dangerous game. One that could ignite a war. "Why did you come here? I know you're not here to challenge birthright?"

Königsmarck and Frida kept flirting with each other from across the way. A smile here, there. Lusty eyes crawling up every wall. Wink, wink.

"I surrender birthright for oath. I challenge Juliette Marquez."

Leonor's silliness and pettiness shocked Mother. "Why would you do something like that?"

"Juliette Marquez stole my love."

What a strange development, Mother pondered. She knew Juliette Marquez well. From a good house. Good child. Star basketball player. Not an evil bone lived underneath that skin.

The House of Carlito and House of Marquez were tight once. Even locked down when the cauldron boiled over. Mother Carlito would never grant Leonor oath. That would cause a war. She would never sanction Juliette Marquez's death. In time, Juliette would be the next Mother.

Something inside Frida snapped. She couldn't believe Leonor would trade a birthright for Tetchy. The part about Juliette Marquez wronging Leonor. Floored her. When Leonor had stolen Tetchy from Frida. Leonor wasn't his first. Not the last. Just part of a bigger group. A chain in the link. Frida furrowed. Eyes narrow as hell. Her voice was commanding. "Tetchy wasn't your love, you know that? He didn't love you. Tetchy is a fuckboy."

Leonor gleamed goblin smack eyes at her. Staring Frida down with those cold brown eyes. "He loved me. I can't say the same to you. You're not a topper."

Mother's eyeballs swirled around inside her head. Frida perched at the edge of the sofa, chest puffed. "Topper?"

Mother squeezed Frida's thigh. "Mother Saramago hasn't granted oath during her reign. Forging a Mother's oath is a serious crime. Death even. The House of Carlito is holy ground. You cannot bleed on holy ground. Lucky you didn't murder my guard, otherwise I could punch your ticket right now. But," she raised a slender finger, "I'm willing to overlook your transgressions under the circumstance. Now," Mother, still clutching Frida's thigh, sat taller, "Mother Saramago is a phone call away. I'll check the facts. If what you say is true."

"Juliette Marquez killed Tetchy. How can you just sit there and do nothing?" Leonor glared at Frida.

"The only person Tetchy ever loved was himself." Frida fluttered her hand. "Face it, Leonor, you're a simp. Not a sidepiece."

Mother squeezed Frida's thigh harder enough to make her grunt. Frida gave Mother a painful look.

Not a soul in the library saw Leonor wriggle free from the handcuffs. Leonor used the sit-down for distraction. When the guards frisked Leonor, they missed something precious. A knife hidden in her boot.

Mother Carlito had more years on Leonor. Fail-safe measures were a key part of the library's design. Had a person planned on killing Mother during a sit-down, the large gold coffee table positioned between the sofas would waste precious time. Its dimensions were beefy and slick. Rounded edges. Taller than the average coffee table by three inches. Measurements matter in cases such as these. A person would need to barrel over a slick piece of furniture to assassinate Mother. Letting Mother enough time fish out a gun, hidden inside a secret compartment, and be done with the whole mess.

Leonor smiled big, almost sadistically. "I lied. Mother Saramago refused my oath. I'm not here to request oath. I'm here to steal oath like I stole Tetchy."

Deep down, fear gripped Königsmarck as the conversation soured. Leonor always gave him the creeps. When nature heads south, it usually means winter is upon them. He edged closer to Frida instead of protecting Mother.

Mother laid her hand on the secret compartment. Lifting the hidden latch as she spoke. "I respect a girl who lives her life the way she pleases. There's only one problem, Leonor."

Leonor wore that priceless expression. Her voice was sweet and snarky. "What's that, Mother Carlito?"

"First oath of Mafia Land." Mother's fingers now gliding over cold metal. "Don't shit where you eat."

The moment Leonor reached for the knife and scaled the coffee table, Königsmarck sprinted toward Frida. In seconds, the knife flew from Leonor's hand and sailed toward Frida. The ultimate kill shot. Before the guards could react, the knife had plunged deep. No, quirky furniture did not save the day. They never theorized an assassin attack. Much less a flying knife.

Leonor had scurried over the coffee table in seconds after throwing the knife. Quick on her feet, Mother Carlito smashed Leonor's nose with the butt of the gun. Leonor was tougher than first assessment and didn't go down. She wore a ready-for-more expression. Mother hit her again. Harder this time. Blood burst from her nose like a bomb. Teeth painted red. Despite that, Leonor had the energy and defiance to smile grander. She giggled madly. Not going down. Rather, up, up, up.

The guards yanked Leonor from the coffee table and restrained her.

Leonor was super quick. Quicker than the guards. Than Mother. But Königsmarck was much quicker. He read her intentions a mile away. Or ten feet. And turned himself into a human shield for the love of his life.

Frida screamed, never-ending. It sounded like a crushed heart. Mother's ears knew the difference between physical pain and heartbreak. The entire time, Mother had focused her attention on Leonor and not Frida.

Mother glanced at Frida. Blood covered parts of Frida as she knelt beside Königsmarck on that silky shag. Inches from where they had smashed just hours ago. Clinging to his hand. Tears in her eyes. Mother was relieved it was Königsmarck, not Frida.

Königsmarck said nothing. His eyes did all the lifting. He kept staring at Frida with that strange look, as though an itch was out of reach. Hand trembling inside hers. Then his body trembled. Blood pooling from his chest. The knife had hit center, way past his lungs. Frida's face spelled confusion. So much blood. It wouldn't stop. His blood would spill in her mind for eternity. Or at the very least, until her premature death.

Within seconds, he stopped quivering. His grip went limp. Eyes fixed on the ceiling.

"Mother!" Frida cried. "Help him."

Mother sat back down. Stunned by the fiasco. Frida couldn't see what Mother saw. Lack of experience noted. Or refusing to stare the truth in the eye. Of what the eye looks like after death. Mother saw something Frida did not. Königsmarck had left the library two seconds ago. In spirit.

Mother Carlito recognized that grave look on her daughter. She had seen it a million times before in Mafia Land. Each death was unique. Some cry. Some laugh. Some scream their little heads off. Some even plead. But they end the same. Every time. When someone punches a ticket, they punch it. Reversing a one way is impossible. Even when someone pays the surcharge.

Juliet • Juliette = Click

Lɪᴀ, the gate attendant, gave Mother Saramago a nervous look. Hesitant to say which Juliet had befallen death. She did her best to muffle the adrenaline. To soften the blow for which she was about to speak. But failed. "It's not Marquez!" Lia motioned to Mother Saramago. "It's Juliet!"

Mother Marquez's heart sank from where she stood in the greenhouse. Who could take a seat under these circumstances? Lia's voice told the story. That tone could only mean one thing: death. Her attendant had delivered her husband's death note in the same tone.

A sense of irony is a funny little beast, Mother Marquez thought. All the whammies. The commotion that surrounds death. They live in fucking Mafia Land. Death notes weren't the exception. It was a guarantee. Blood in, blood out. Why was everyone so shocked when death found its mark? As though it wasn't supposed to go this way. There's always someone dying in Mafia Land. Death note is a way of life.

That grave expression never fell away. Yes, deep down, Mother Marquez was relieved to hear Juliette was safe. *Juliette and Juliet may not know love*, Mother Marquez thought. *But Juliette will soon learn the dark hand of love.* Now, her daughter would feel the diseased side. The unlivable side.

Mother Saramago swayed, as though the floor had vanished. Her eyes fluttered. Her hands trembled while gravitating toward her mouth. Mother Marquez rushed to Mother Saramago and grabbed her arm to stabilize, thinking she might pass out from shock.

Mother Marquez peered at Lia. "Was it Leonor?"

Lia kept focus on Mother Saramago. "No."

"Then who, girl?"

Lia was too frightened to reveal whatever was left to tell.

"Who did it?"

"She did."

"What about Juliette?"

All Mother Saramago could think was that Juliet was a quiet child. Silent as a zinger. Beware of the quiet ones. To think, the first story to barrel from Juliet's mouth was love. Mother Saramago was still trembling. "The gun." And collapsed.

Lia and Mother rushed to Mother Saramago's aid. After all this time, a party of death would gather once more. Different time. Same people. Mother Saramago understood Mafia Land's tales of heartbreak masked a harsher reality.

Moments later, Lia had revived Mother Saramago. She had finally come to after administering zinger blood. They kneeled. Peering down at her with worried eyes. Mother Saramago woke crying. "I can't. I just can't."

Mother held Mother Saramago's face still. "Listen to me. I know this devastation. It gets easier." Mother Marquez's eyes darted as though she were ready to cry, too. She could barely believe those cruel words had spilled from her lips. Because she knew it never got easier. It never, ever gets easier. So, why say it at all?

* * *

One by one, attendants and guards trailed behind Mother Saramago. Mother Marquez and Lia were by her side as they marched. Soon, as word spread throughout Mafia Land, everyone headed for the Sacred Arch to bear witness to this tragedy.

Mother Marquez could hear whimpers and whispers rippling through the crowd. She heard Juliet's name spoken several times. But she couldn't be sure which Juliet. Mother Saramago wore a stone face. Ears boarded up. She had closed shop to Mafia Land while tears plummeted. Eyes checked out, no place left to run.

When they finally arrived at the Sacred Arch, Sister Claude stood guard. Her sad eyes looking onward to some place not on the map. Everybody was wearing sad eyes, no matter where Lia looked. Eyes darting to the ground or elsewhere. Half-lit or cashed. Not cashed by death, just exhausted from trauma. Death is a tiresome business.

Mother Marquez could see Juliette lying next to Juliet Saramago on the blue stone. She clung to Juliet's body as though she were dangling off a cliff. Too afraid to let go. Afraid to let love fall from her fingertips.

The scene was graver than first imagined. Juliette had a gun in her hand. At first, Mother Marquez wondered why Juliette's blood-soaked hands were shining in the suns. But once they closed in, the gun came into full view. The blood pooling was too much to bear.

Mother Marquez shuttered to hear those cries come from her daughter. Juliette wailed heartbreak with a gun in her hand. What was she going to do with it? Mother Marquez wanted to know. Fear stopped her from asking. To agitate a sensitive situation. To dismantle a bomb.

A Mother knows when a child can take no more. Reaches the end of the road. With no heart to go any further. Boxed in like a scared baba foot.

Lia broke from the crowd and edged closer to Juliette. Lia hadn't noticed Sister Claude shaking her head. Waving her hands not to come any closer. A devastating aerial crash was about to happen. Despite how bad the odds were in Mafia Land, Sister Claude believed she could save Juliette.

Juliette sprung and pointed the gun. "Get away!"

Gasps filtered through the crowd. Someone screamed.

Lia held out her hands. "We just want to help." She slowly backed away, as though staring down at the eyes of a goblin smack.

Juliette then aimed the gun at her head.

Another person screamed.

Juliette stared at Mother, finger on the trigger. "I can't anymore, not without Juliet."

Questions: If a heart breaks once, does the second time hurt less? Or does it hurt twice as much? Are stages of pain levels to master like a video game?

Mother Marquez had only screamed once in her life. Otherwise, she was stoic to the bone. Even during the gravest times. She screamed when she'd received her husband's head. And now.

Mother Saramago snapped out of it. Not for her Juliet. But for Marquez. She would stop the bloodshed, no matter what. Her voice was gentle as silk. Her hands spread out. "You know Juliet wouldn't have wanted this. She loved you." Poor choice of words at a time like this. She made the fatal mistake of using past tense.

Juliette peered down at Juliet's lifeless body. If only the crowd could have seen that she had decided. Juliet's flesh was turning pale and waxy. Eyes half-lit, as though dozing. Merley dozing. But Juliette knew the difference. She had dined on death before.

Juliet's skin was icicles. Hugging Juliet was like hugging iron. Her Juliet was never coming back. That was that. "You're my all." She faced the onlookers, closed her eyes, and pulled the trigger. Everyone in the crowd gasped loud enough to reach the stratosphere.

Instead of a loud bang, the gun spewed a dull click. All the eyes upon her now, looking surprised and relieved in one swoop. Especially Mother Marquez. Surprise seized Juliette, too. Not the outcome she had hoped for. A woman in the crowd sighed. "Oh, thank goodness."

Mother Marquez peered back to whoever in the crowd had said that. She wanted to lock eyes on the woman who says thank goodness in a time such as this. She chilled after seeing the countless faces of anguish. The grief-stricken.

The dull click of the gun didn't faze. Juliette was determined to join Juliet in the underworld. Or any life thereafter. She pulled the trigger again to hear another haunting click. Then again, click. The gun would deliver nothing. She stared at the crowd, tears spilling. Just when the bad part seemed over, Juliette's eyes went wacky. Then lackadaisical. Then, for some odd reason, she clawed at her chest, as though she were having a heart attack. She stared at the crowd, panicked, like she was suffocating. All her insides cashing chips. Her knees liquefied, and she crumbled to the floor wearing a frozen, horrified look.

Everyone thought she had passed out from the shock. But after Sister Claude checked her pulse and performed CPR, Juliette Marquez had died of a broken heart. Once the medics arrived to confirm what everyone in the crowd already knew, it was too late. Juliette wasn't coming back. Never.

Juliet and Juliette were living on borrowed time. Especially Juliette Marquez. Catalepsy had taken care of that. Her heart had stopped on a dime. The Good Book already recorded that Juliette Marquez would die of a weak heart at two thirty-three today. Some claim a broken heart. It raises the question: does it matter which of the two ended Juliette? Her heart stopped. Class dismissed.

Although dying of a broken heart is more probable than the former. Broken heart syndrome, also known as stress-induced cardiomyopathy, kills 8 percent a year. A healthy heart can stop beating under stressful circumstances. One can only guess what happens to a weak heart under catastrophic circumstances. One being, losing the love of your life. Love can cause the heart to skip a beat. Or end every single beat for all time.

They say death waits for no one. Including love. That statement has a condition. One cannot shove death down the stairs because it crawls. Death is neither early nor late. Tolling the hours like an atomic clock. No matter who pulls the trigger.

Hours later, they sat in the greenhouse wearing faces of sorrow. War lost to the lost. Now, and somehow, they must surrender themselves to whatever was left. Hunched in their seats as though the true weight of Mafia Land rested on them. Despite their vacant stares, Mother Saramago secretly believed this was a nightmare. She'd wake soon.

Deep in thought, Mother Marquez furrowed her brows. Replaying the day's events. She turned toward Lia. "Why didn't you leave her alone? You made this happen."

Lia didn't make eye contact. Instead, she fixed her eyes straight ahead, somewhere out in the yonder. Chin resting inside her palms, as though she were bored. "My bad."

That stubborn sore throat returned as Mother Marquez messaged her neck. Mother Saramago gestured weakly to the attendant. "Platinum elixir, whipper sweets biscuit."

The attendant gave a look of concern. "What can I get you?"

"Juliet." Mother Saramago never made eye contact. Her dreamlike voice said it all. "Tell Juliet to come down here. I'd like to speak with her about something."

"Mother?"

Mother Marquez and Lia both glared at the attendant. Mother Marquez shook her head and shooed him, mouthing, "just go."

Mafia Land is big, yet the size of a quark, as noted prior. Everyone knew the latest gossip. News traveled at light speed. Damn those algorithms and surveillance devises. A gate attendant rushed into the greenhouse, almost tripping on her way in. "Mother Carlito is at the gate. She's requesting a sit-down."

Mother Marquez rested her forehead in her hands and mumbled, "Enough with the son-of-a-bitchin' sit-downs."

"They captured Leonor and handed her over to the arena police."

Hearing Leonor's name burned a hole through the heart with a sprinkle of radioactive salt. *This had all started over Leonor and Tetchy's love affair. This is all Leonor's fault,* Mother Saramago thought. *And Tetchy. That little pricky prick.* Still, she says the only thing she can. "Let them in."

Mother Saramago, somewhere deep down, acknowledged her failure. She had invited Leonor into the House of Saramago. Leonor's bloodline was from the old world. She knew better than to mix spoiled meat with fresh.

When Mother Carlito entered the garden room, she was not alone. She had brought her entourage. Several attendants and guards. Most were carrying gifts and flowers. The heart, like the weather, changes rapidly. Furious rain pelted the greenhouse with a clamorous patter as though a thousand snares had landed at once. The sky turned black.

Mother Carlito strode into the greenhouse like royalty. Not to pay respects, but to celebrate a merger through marriage. She ordered the attendants and guards to sprinkle the room with gifts. An exotic feast lie before. Endangered elixirs. Goblin smack heart, a rare delicacy. Tundra caviar from the Isle of Rubia. The skin of a glass-newt, an aphrodisiac of the gods. They spared no expense. It all existed. Including blood from the zinger. One attendant swung a gold censer. Permeating the room with aromatic incense and white smoke. Charcoal and cypress. The room smelled like a burned forest.

In Mafia Land, they hold wedding rituals to honor star-crossed lovers who die before the Art of Rubia takes place. Death can stop the heart. But cannot stop love. Love is timeless. Love is a good death.

Mother Carlito brought the ritual to the House of Saramago. Instead of hosting. Which was a great honor. She certified the marriage. Mafia Land still mourned. Rightfully, so. However, death-wedding celebrations were loud enough to reach the afterlife.

Mother Carlito paid her respects. Kissed Mother Saramago on the cheek. Whispered something in her ear that Lia overheard. Mother Saramago turned and said, "Grant me oath as a last request."

Inside Mother Saramago's head, she whispered it. In reality, she had shouted. Anyone in the vicinity heard what she had said. Mother Marquez was sitting the closest. "This isn't the time to settle things in your condition."

"That, I won't allow."

"You refuse my oath?"

The story enthralled Mother Marquez and scooting two inches closer.

"I granted oath to someone else."

"Whose oath is more powerful than mine?"

"Frida has challenged Leonor."

Mother Marquez puckered her face. "My goodness."

Mother Saramago shook her head. "I cannot bear to see another future Mother die at the hands of that girl."

"It's done. That's tradition."

"For Tetchy," Mother Marquez said while adjusting.

"For Königsmarck."

"Who the hell is Königsmarck?"

"If you don't rescind that oath, you will sign your daughter's death note. Frida will die in the arena, mark my words. Don't forget about the omen. Frida would make number three. Children die in threes."

Mother Carlito scoffed. "You and your silly superstitions."

"We did this." Mother Saramago whipped her finger in a circle. Linking the Mothers with a simple gesture. "Our sins are catching up."

"Look around," Mother Marquez said. "Girls can be whatever they want. They're not afraid of men anymore. Men no longer decide a woman's future in Mafia Land because of us."

"You're right," Mother Saramago said, sadness in her eyes. "We make the final decision. But we're no different. The proof is all around. You only need to look."

Mother Carlito's voice was razor sharp. "Enough!"

Mother Saramago stood and glared at Mother Carlito, then Mother Marquez for ten seconds too long. "I'm tired." She straightened her track suit. "I won't celebrate my daughter's death."

Nine Lives of Boomer

ANCIENT COLOSSEUMS INSPIRED the design of the arena. Plenty of seats and crystal-clear acoustics fed people who hungered for justice. Some craved blood and carnage more.

Anyone could challenge anyone, except for the Mothers. No one could challenge them. Not everyone agreed with the bureaucracy that surrounded fight for life. A group of citizens even tried to enact legal loopholes to stop the barbaric practice, with little success.

Once challenged, a contestant could not refuse to participate. They had to fight to the death. Some who protested the grisly event escaped the city after they had sworn an oath to fight. A small population disappeared without a trace.

So, the Mothers created a sophisticated legal system that included secret police. They even built a futuristic prison in the coliseum's basement. The justice system jailed anyone considered a flight risk. And those who committed a violent crime. The secret police guarded the contestant until fight for life. They expedited the process. Once convicted of a crime, the contestant would bleed to death in the arena within a couple of days.

It wasn't as though fight for life was being held each time the suns rose every six hours. Not anymore, anyway. Initially, sure. After a year, people on the winning side lost their taste for blood and revenge. In most challenges, they granted oaths against contestants who committed heinous or violent acts.

* * *

Mother Carlito may have fired shots at Mother Saramago. But she heeded those words. Mother Saramago told the truth. In Mafia Land, children die in threes. The omen never lies. Mother Saramago correctly declared their fate sealed. The sins of the past never go unpunished.

In Mafia Land, Mothers are the ultimate authority. To achieve their goals, sometimes Mothers must strike a bargain with the devil. Even sign a life or two away. Placing your life in the devil's hands is another uncertainty. One should condemn the devil's idea of repayment. It will always fall short of expectations.

Leonor lay sprawled on the couch. Feet propped on a coffee table. She was chewing while balancing a bowl in her hand. When Mother Carlito entered the arena prison, she watched Leonor for a while. The last time Leonor was in proximity, she had tried to punch Frida's ticket.

At a safe distance, Leonor looked as innocent as a zebra fawn. Behaving like any other day. Mother Carlito had to tell herself the girl had killed Königsmarck hours ago. The bottom of Leonor's feet were black. As though she had trampled through a pit of ash. Still, she looked broken. Like a child who had lost its mother. Mother Carlito wanted to scoop her up and whisk her away to a better place. She was fooling herself, though. Leonor found her perfect place. One could say she was more comfortable than a zinger dillydallying in the forest.

Mother Carlito snuck up behind her. Leonor still eating. Unaware, Mother Carlito was standing two feet away, watching every move. "Can I sit?"

Leonor continued to chew. Mother Carlito's presence did not startle her. She didn't even flinch. Leonor stared ahead, eating cereal like a kid hypnotized by cartoons. She moved over a few inches. "It's your place." Leonor's mouth was full.

It wasn't until Mother sat she noticed the tears. Leonor's eyes were puffy, as though she had been crying all day. Mother Carlito's body language was fight-or-flight. She would not let her guard down for a second. Her life depended on it. "There's no reason to continue this charade. Those you wish dead are dead."

Mother waited for Leonor to say something. Did Leonor regret her actions? Mother wanted to know. She could see Leonor had feelings because she was crying. Who could say to what degree, though? Leonor's tears could be goblin smack tears. Mother knew she was no zebra fawn.

"Why did you try to punch Frida's ticket?"

Leonor stopped chewing. She set the bowl on the coffee table and chucked the spoon with a loud clink. Then shrugged. "Can I trust you?" Mother stirred her hand fast, like stirring stew. "Give me your word and I'll rescind."

This was the first time Mother Carlito had handed someone a get-out-of-jail card. Leonor was silent and clear as ice. She wouldn't take the deal. Tears trickled down her cheeks. That blank stare afterburner.

"You don't care if you live or die, do you?"

People say that for a greater chance of success, you must put all your energy into plan A. Devise plan B on the fly. After plan A backfires. If one should place more focus on B, rather than A, then A will fail.

Mother Carlito took a different approach. Less desirable. Plan B was to convince Leonor to rescind oath. Even though they granted Frida oath first. Frida wanted to avenge Königsmarck. But would she perish during battle.

Plan A was much darker. Mother Carlito had smuggled a dagger inside the arena prison, tucked under her sleeve. If things soured. If Leonor refused to back down. Leonor was a trained assassin. Most likely the deadliest in Mafia Land. Mother Carlito had little doubt Frida would prevail.

Heeding Mother Saramago's advice, Mother Carlito regretted granting Frida oath. *What the hell was I thinking?* She had wondered. Still, Mother Sarámago's words haunted as she sat beside Leonor. Those words rang like a deadly bell that stops the heart. Mother Carlito was trying like hell to reverse the clock.

Mother Carlito overlooked an important detail. Leonor was lightning-fast. She had iced Königsmarck in seconds. Mother Carlito wasn't as fast. She couldn't compete at this level. Perhaps in her thirties, she could.

"What are you waiting for?" Leonor leaned back, hands at her side. "Get on with it."

Mother Carlito's heart slammed against her chest doing a hundred. Blood pressure blown to hell. Rage surging through the pipes. Sweat beading on her forehead.

Leonor leaned farther back. More relaxed than before. Hands resting behind her head. Dirty feet on solid ground. Waiting for Mother Carlito to strike.

When Mother Carlito felt cold steel in her hand, she thrust the dagger with all her weight. It plunged deeper than expected. It almost got swallowed up.

For the first time since the conversation had begun, Leonor finally showed emotion. She grunted like a cheetah mule. Winched a strange expression, as though conflicted by the blow. It wasn't supposed to be this painful.

She didn't put up a fight. *Why didn't she put up a fight?* Now that they were super close. Almost nose to nose. An intimate kill swam about. Leonor's breath smelled like platinum elixir. Her skin bore the scent of whipper sweets. She smelled like wildflowers in a meadow. Something that traced back to the House of Saramago.

Their gazes met. Leonor's face was twitchy. Her eyes quivered as though she was trying to warm to a knife having plunged deep. Mother Carlito saw Leonor enduring the blow. Even absorbing it. "Fight back, girl. Don't you want to live?"

That evil smile and casual tone implied something more sinister was afoot. Mother Carlito's gut turned at that moment. She knew she had fucked up.

"You forgot the rules. Now I can kill you legally. An eye for an eye, remember?" Leonor kissed Mother Carlito on the lips. "Once I'm done with you, I'm goanna kill your daughter. *Very* slowly."

Mother Carlito's eyes rose, horror-stricken. "You evil bitch."

Leonor ripped the dagger from her side with another grunt. The blade had nicked her hip bone. Mother Carlito struggled with the knife, but not fast enough.

With one stroke of the blade, Leonor slit Mother Carlito's jugular. Assassin style. Leonor had out gangsta'd a gangster.

Everything had happened so fast, Mother Carlito's brain couldn't catch up. She had not felt the blade glide across her throat. Much less cut deep. The blood trickled down her neck. She felt warm droplets splash on her collarbone. Then the blood fanned out. Mother Carlito clutched her neck and made an odd gurgling noise. "Aughhh… aughhh…aughhh…aughhh."

Extreme blood loss knocked Mother Carlito forward. With little control, she slumped against Leonor. Leonor gave a look of disgust. She shoved Mother Carlito away as if she had a deadly virus.

Mother Carlito refused to die. Leonor could hear her gasping against the cushion. Still clinging to life. Leonor stood to watch Mother Carlito bleed out. When paralyzing pain exploded near the hip. "Aww." She pinched the wound closed, but blood poured between her fingers. "Shit."

She hadn't expected Mother Carlito could deliver this blow. It appeared they had underestimated each other. They didn't do their homework. The blade went deeper than she had thought. Much deeper. The blood sifting through her fingers was as dark as death. She took a few brief steps to flag down arena police, then collapsed. Blood gushed from her hip like a faucet.

"Help," she said, but her ears were ringing. Her head was buzzing. "Help." Her entire body burst with violent tingles, as though her muscles had fallen asleep. Each time she cried for help, in her head, it sounded like a roar.

All her senses malfunctioned. What came out were whispers. Soon, her body went numb. The pain fell away. The ground was icy, but she couldn't feel the difference. Laying on the floor felt soothing. Eyes adrift. Rolling around somewhere out in the yonder.

* * *

Leonor Saramago was Ferrante first. Uncle Stigmata had had the taxing responsibility of raising Addy and Leonor after their parents had died during the long war.

Uncle Stigmata had seen promise in her early on. He had a specific job in mind for her. To train Leonor in the assassin's ways. He saw no promise in Addy and shipped her off to Whitehead.

Uncle Stigmata had difficulty conforming to Mafia Land. The Mothers drove him to the brink. Especially their ways. Their ideals are more accurate than anything else. They were old school. Lugging the old ways around town before Mafia Land was Mafia Land. *What's the difference between Mafia Land and Land of Kings, absolutely nothing,* he thought. But he had the power to return the land to its rightful place.

Before Mafia Land, another kingdom had existed. These men of kings controlled every part of a woman's life. Women didn't hold positions of power. Not inside their homes. No where. These kings prevented women from voting. Mind, body, and soul belonged to the state. And the men who ran the state.

Men ran politics. They were the instructors at the colleges. They taught K-12. They were doctors and scientists and mathematicians. Men decided what women could do with their bodies. Men flew the transits. Built the cities and houses. Ran the banking institutions. Designed the laws. Tailored women's apparel. Even their undergarments and hygiene products. Taught sex education, etc.

In the Land of Kings, even their god was a man. Religious holograms filled with men—prophets and leaders and miracle workers and kings and more kings. In these religious virtual realities, women were the evildoers. Every algorithm written, and available to the public, had a common theme. Men were the heroes and explorers and dreamers and thinkers and inventors. Men were the moral compasses and knowledge givers. In most stories, women were the foes and witches and spell casters and tempters. Women were feebleminded and weak. Not damsels in distress, rather anchors on society. Anchors to a ship. Necessary equipment through choppy waters. One small hunk of metal could sink a ship if not tracked and maintained. Temperamental things break and cause a lot of damage. If one turns their back for one second.

That all changed after the long war ended. Mothers overthrew king rule. Even after the long war had ended, Uncle Stigmata found it difficult to live his life as accustomed. Under new management.

The old ways cauterized his brain. He had no children of his own. Boys might have helped him, but adding girls to his responsibilities sealed his fate.

Uncle Stigmata flaunted his wealth every chance he got. He wore three-piece suits made of the finest wool. Every day of his life. Even during the summer months. Tailored lines and angles that represented a different decade. A much older decade.

He wasn't trying to step back in time. He had never left. That slicked-back hair was drowning in oil, as though he had jumped out of the shower. Sporting a gray fade that ran away years ago and never looked backed. Still, he was a daddy. If there ever was one. He'd be the one, to everyone's dismay.

Uncle Stigmata's manifesto was best summed up as this: a woman should never stumble into bad lighting. All four suns. The suns revealed everything. Undesirable things. To a trained eye. Beauty was beholden by a man. For example, a widow peak or smoker's crease or spider reach could shine brighter than all the suns. A spider reach could age a woman by ten years, he had claimed. "Light, my dear. Be wary of the light."

Uncle Stigmata despised shadows. Shadows crept along the face. Flesh laid over bone. Revealed undesirable details. Arm hair. Fuzzy upper lips and jawlines. One must mitigate a woman's hair at all costs. One must keep hair in its proper place. No hair was best. Except for the head and brow and down below. *Women are not primates*, he stated. Female primates had hair because they couldn't shave themselves. *It's impossible, it's all in the wrist.*

Controlled lighting saved the day. He introduced the girls to a warm LED. Soft LED. Blue LED. *Always walk under these lights*, he instructed. If one could help it. When one could help it. And, by one, he meant them or women. Flattery, under perfect lighting, was a woman's best defense. Her best attributes.

Smell was at the top of his list of things to mitigate. Menstrual cycles were troublesome. The scent of a woman. The *actual* scent of a woman. He must mask it. Engineered or artificial. Didn't matter. Perfumes eliminate foul odors. Was the standard to reach. Even if a lady needed to roll around in a vat of chemical solutions to permeate the skin or what have you. A woman's natural scent should radiate the lovely note of raspberries. It's not a woman's fault. Evolution royally fucked up. According to Uncle Stigmata. And needed tweaking before the guests arrived for the dinner.

His other obsession was time. *Use time well. Spend time in productive ways.* Efficient as a nuclear clock. But counting one's time could be curt. Ending a good time before the baba foot hatched was a downer. Missing a once-in-a-lifetime phenomenon that only happened every seventy-five thousand years.

As luck would have it. Uncle Stigmata charted the constellations and found Leonor was born under a rare astrological event. The goblin smack star. Now, Kele, Leonor's father, should have named her after that star. But he didn't. Uncle Stigmata never let Leonor forget that.

Uncle Stigmata believed, with all his heart and soul, that Leonor was the second coming. Not a female, but as good as any boy out there. He trained her like an assassin. Any father, brand new or not, would. A boy must learn how to fight. How to protect themselves. How to get themselves out of a jam while icing five men. Ten was best. Ten was the bar to reach.

Before retirement, Uncle Stigmata had worked for the state. The deep state. Where he trained men to kill in their sleep. If need be.

Problem solving was not part of the training. Nor necessary. Uncle Stigmata surmised smart assassins were troublesome. Even tiresome to everyone around. They thought too much during the battle. Smart assassins eventually turned on their masters.

He wasn't training scientists or astronauts. He was training killing machines. Whose sole purpose was to kill. Or to be killed. This thinking doomed the long war. Nobody clued Uncle Stigmata in on that little secret.

The strict practice of time is an illusion. It's like trying to capture air and seal it in a bottle. Air always finds a way out. Not in. Time has no master. Time moves differently throughout the cosmos. Sometimes, not all. Time doesn't exist everywhere.

Addy was a genius. Which went against Uncle Stigmata's strict set of rules. Plus, her hands were too small to fire a gun. Too small to choke a man to death. "No, no, no. You won't do. Not in the least." Uncle Stigmata had slapped her hands away in disgust.

The best thing to do with a girl of her pedigree, as though she were a baba foot, was to ship her off to Whitehead until her premature death.

He had trained Leonor like he would any man. Over time, Uncle Stigmata realized something groundbreaking. Females were cleverer than men. Not just clever but adaptable, pliable. A girl can flex her body in many ways. Able to squeeze into tight spaces. Springing from the rafter through the ventilation system had never crossed his mind. A man could never fit. Even if he could, his mechanics or flexibility would never match a girl. Yes, Uncle Stigmata discovered girls were far better assassins than boys. He pointed to the sky, boasting, "I created the perfect killing machine." As if he had invented electricity.

Uncle Stigmata had trained Leonor for one purpose. To assassinate the Mothers. All the mothers. The works. Leonor had shipped Sorus Saramago's head, Mother Saramago's husband, through Amazon. Gold tissue paper. The works. She had assassinated him and made it look as though Mother Marquez did it. The plan succeeded.

Mother Saramago returned the gesture with a personal touch. Handed Bruno Marquez, Mother Marquez's husband, a death note.

When things heated, and the Mothers prepared for war, the plan ran out of juice in rush-hour traffic. Mother Carlito's flying limo had died on the I-101. Leonor waited inside the ventilation system at a swanky restaurant bathroom. Armed and ready to assassinate. But Mother Carlito never arrived.

Uncle Stigmata knew his enemy little. The Mothers were best friends since childhood. Kings no longer ruled the land. Mother Saramago and Mother Marquez were 4lifers. After phone calls, texts and surveillance footage, later squashed the feud. The Mothers learned of his plan and prevented his return.

Had it not been for Mother Carlito's flying limo getting stranded on the I-101, the plan might have worked.

* * *

Before retirement, Uncle Stigmata and a coworker wrote a nine-page document claiming women are too emotional for power. The manifesto claimed women are ineffective and dangerous leaders because of their emotional decision-making. Women do not use their brains when making informed decisions. Instead, they let their emotions do the lifting. Especially during certain times of the month. The hypothesis dedicated one page to the claim that a woman's menstrual cycle could cause a world war.

What they had not acknowledged. Land of Kings was always at war with some faction. War was profitable. War was an excuse to take precious resources from another land. The thinking was this: whoever had weapons of mass destruction was king. Which birthed the saying: for god, for gold, for glory. They usually omitted the reference to god.

People praised Uncle Stigmata for his groundbreaking manifesto. However, they underestimated these so-called foreign agents. They didn't know how cunning women could be at politics. Far more superior to their counterparts. Contrary to nonsensical belief, that strategy was their downfall. It seemed Uncle Stigmata never accounted for every possibility. They were too busy underestimating women.

Women had endured since time was time. The Land of Kings' fall was inevitable. Every woman knew it. They knew freedom would rise over the mountain scape one day soon. Sometimes one must burn the village to the ground to start fresh. The Mothers succeeded. Class dismissed.

Small Men = Small God

In the Land of Kings, females could not pursue education. Their sole responsibilities lay in motherhood. A good wife was determined by a man. Academic technology was off-limits to every female. Or any interactive hologram that was state certified for a man.

The banned-technology list grew every year. Enough to fill every quantum database in the land. Its growth persisted. The State Department basement overflowed with volumes of holographic data storage. The law shielded females from harmful ideas. Hung countless that dare defy the law. Mostly, women. Occasionally, children.

To prevent women from reading forbidden literature, the state built special libraries. They were minimal. Five hundred square feet on the dot. One for each community. Some communities only had a closet-sized library.

But in the eyes of the state, that measure wasn't extreme enough. One never knows what might tempt a corruptible mind. "Start when they're young" was the buzzword idea. State members, including Charity Adams, created a K-12 all-girls' school named after the founding father, Charity Adams.

Charity Adams's school days were only three hours and fifteen minutes. The state had banned so many subjects. They considered dance, art, early childhood mathematics, and language arts safe. Not completely safe, but less troublesome. Sophomore year, the school added home economics to the syllabus for adolescent girls.

* * *

The state employed Leonor's father, Kele Stigmata, as a computer scientist. A gifted one at that. Despite its oppression, the Land of Kings was technologically advanced.

Leonor's mother, Mika, was a self-taught botanist. Educating herself through forbidden literature. Supplied by Kele. He was the complete opposite of his brother, Uncle Stigmata. Far from a state sympathizer. Kele believed women deserved the same rights as men, including education.

Kele educated Mika, Leonor and Addy in secret. Knowing full well the family would hang in the square if word ever got out. He wasn't the only person who thought women deserved equal rights. A growing number of men broke state laws to educate. They began holding meetings at odd hours of the night. Men from various backgrounds planned a coup against the State Department.

Women found an education loophole. In the Land of Kings, females of all ages, including infants, had to exercise. The word of the day was *robust*. The State Department wanted strong women throughout the land. They built sprawling fitness centers. Indoor pools. Indoor everything. No expense spared. These were the only organizations managed by women. The State Department prohibited men from accessing the fitness centers.

At first, women complied. What choice did they have? They swam laps. Ran track. Lifted weights. Yoga the hell out of those bods. Did all the things the State Department required them to do. To become: ROBUST AND BEAUTIFUL as the banner read. Every fitness center in the land displayed the same banner in its entryway.

Three women organized a revolt against the state. Inside a fitness center. Not all revolts were violent. Some of the greatest revolts had humble beginnings. All shared a common denominator.

Their motivation stemmed from a desire to end their oppressive misery.

In Mountain Region, the Mothers oversaw the fitness center, which later became known as the House of Carlito. They weren't sisters by blood but tight as sisters—4lifers.

They were fond of crafting elixirs and exotic oils and plants that healed the body. Healed the skin. The mind. Their potions and pills worked. Better than anything a woman could buy in a drugstore. Any store in the land. Who knows a woman's body better than a woman?

The Mothers' potions become known. Their fitness center got very popular. Women and girls flooded into the center. Coming and going at all hours. No longer getting robust but healed. Injuries and illnesses, once believed incurable, now cured.

Their elixirs and pills worked like magic. Some accused them of practicing alchemy. Others thought they were witches. Knowledge is power in most circles, but not. In the days of old. Scientific knowledge was witchcraft.

To practice alchemy within the constructs of reason was one thing. But the practice of sedition was a more deadly offense. To conspire against the state, may god save the souls who dared.

* * *

Elixirs can't heal every item on the list. Many exceptions complicated the process. They required medical holograms and more botany algorithms. State-level technology. Knowledge from the highest order. That's like asking the gods to pass down their knowledge.

They added a fourth member to the group. A botanist named Mikki. She kept her identity a secret. The four began their mission to heal the wounded. The broken. The infirm. As history shows, the laws of oppression are on borrowed time. But don't crumble quick enough.

* * *

There's something to be said about the human desire to reach the heavens after death. If there is a God, does God care about human affairs? God is, well, God. And humans are, well, not.

If god is nothing more than human invention. The greatest invention ever. Created to keep the masses in check. It raises the question, wouldn't a human god share the same flaws as its creator?

Was the creation of god one of those fake-it-till-you-make-it sort of deals? Or fake it until they believe? Either by beheading or hanging or by some other tortuous end?

Let's suppose one lacks imagination. Or a brain. What do you suppose that god would seem like? Small minds drum up small things. The founding father, Charles Chancellor, was one of those people.

* * *

Charles despised hard work. Of any kind. He never vacuumed. Never made a bed. Did the dishes. Filthy dishes piled up on both sides of the sink. On every horizontal surface sat a dirty dish. If the latest leftovers could line the ceiling, he'd find a way. Everywhere the eyes roamed inside that four hundred-square-foot apartment landed on filth.

Cups and forks and bowls and butter knives and plates of various sizes, even saucers, infested with mold and bacteria. Teams of slithers built colonies upon those crumbs from the latest meal. Horned flies swarmed around like a blabber hoof pasture.

The state of his apartment was uninhabitable. Something the State Department would condemn. If they caught wind. The smell of rotting things lurking didn't faze him one iota. He didn't even hold his breath when entering his shoebox apartment after taking a stroll. It mattered little that the fresh air had filled his nostrils seconds ago. He couldn't distinguish between the living and the dead.

The smell of dead things lurking behind every corner had desensitized him. Strangely, his apartment was at war with his appearance. He always left the house godly intact. Pressed and pristine. Hair flawless and manicured above ears. Fingernails buffed. Under certain light, they bore a professional sheen. White, fresh teeth. Mustache waxed and curled toward the suns.

Charles had no formal education. Convinced himself he wouldn't find a decent career without one. Despite his dashing appearance, he had tried many occupations. A laborer. A server. A dishwasher—one can imagine how that went. Medical courier. He enjoyed the medical courier position best. The work was effortless. But he kept getting pulled over for speeding. The speeding tickets piled up. They fired him after his twenty-first ticket. He was no longer insurable.

Calling Charles talentless would be a massive understatement. The only success he found was in the military. He was skilled at killing. He could read the battlefield. Sniff out the poor formations and weak men. Yet, no soldier dare follow him into battle. Here's the thing about war: if you can't trust your fellow soldier, then who the hell can you trust?

Twelve days into combat training, Charles couldn't shine a boot. He slapped wax all over those dreadful, mud-caked boots. He couldn't figure out why the damn things wouldn't come to a mirror shine. A fellow soldier had mentioned how he polished boots like he polished his ass. Which was never adequate. Or up to snuff. Not for military standards. The military would have booted him out on his ass. If they started grading how well people polished their, you know.

After receiving his fourth and final reprimand, he did the unthinkable. He traded those mud-caked boots for shiny ones. He had spied them sitting next to a footlocker. He stole his bunkmate's boots without a second thought. Like many things in his life, he was a sloppy thief, too. Another recruit had seen Charles make the swap. From that day on, they labeled Charles as the enemy on the wrong side of the battlefield.

All that negative hype did not detour his impulses. He continued to fudge the system. Stealing extra portions at mealtime. Stealing underwear, toothbrushes, paperclips. He even stole a picture of someone's sweetheart. Everyone in the barracks knew he was a thief. They tried to bolt everything down, but somehow, he stole more.

Each time he cleaned the communal toilets, he suffered from

stomach flu. Whenever the platoon received a task, he fucked off. The platoon had had enough. And pleaded with their sergeant, considering the evidence, to kick Charles out of the military.

Remember this: one can be terrible at a lot of things. Downright awful. But successful at one. Better than all the rest. That one thing can save one's ass. In Charles's case, that was the case. If war is something one should be good at.

The only time his team could count on him was on the battlefield. He was a true killer. He told everyone he heard the voice of God. God instructed him on how to win the war. Though most of his fellow soldiers thought he was full of shit. They knew he loved the kill more. They were right. Charles reveled in the battlefield's stench. The gunpowder. The explosions. The agonizing pain. The sounds of bullets whizzing by his face brought tears of joy. The screams a man makes when he's gutted or decapitated.

Charles realized his destiny had come full circle. Home wasn't that four-hundred-square-foot apartment. Not the park he strolled most every day at ten. The bakery he visited at six. For fresh popals filled with raspberry jelly. The line of customers stretched around the corner beforehand. Home, in his heart, was the battlefield. Straight to the heart, home was where human suffrage lived.

* * *

His father had passed when he was eleven. His mother, lacking an education, worked three jobs to keep the family afloat. Laundry, cooking, and scrubbing toilets were how she kept the family fed. She was the hired help in some of the richest households in the land. When they fell on hard times, she rented out a room to a sales traveler. His childhood home was double the size of his apartment. Two small bedrooms and a toilet. The living room doubled as a kitchen.

Charles and his younger brother slept on the couch. The sales traveler occupied their childhood bedroom. The sales traveler was a unique person. He sold holy digital tablets ordained by Magistrate

Eusebius. Which was like buying a digital tablet from God. From God's lips to your ears. Then to the soul. Then to poverty.

However, a problem existed. Magistrate Eusebius had never ordained the sales traveler's holy tablets. Magistrate Eusebius only gave his blessing to statesmen. They tortured and mutilated anyone caught defying that law. Most people prayed for death after Magistrate Eusebius got done with them.

Still, that didn't detour the sales traveler from supplying a certificate of authenticity with every purchase. A counterfeit certificate he made inside the bedroom he rented. He was a master at forging state seals. Which seemed to catch the eye of Charles.

Charles's childhood neighborhood was best described as a den of thieves. Liquor stores and bars sat on every corner. Drug dealers and pimps ran the streets. Petty thieves and vandals roamed. Graffiti sprayed on the sides of high-speed-rail cars and air buses and alleyways.

Life was miserable for the family. Charles was miserable. His younger brother saw nothing wrong with life among the den of thieves. While walking home from school, his brother shouted, "Life is great, isn't it?"

His brother said this after filching a candy bar from a broken vending machine. *No*, Charles thought. *Life isn't great. It's far from great.* If stealing a candy bar from a vending machine was as good as it got, then he would rather throw himself off a bridge. Or jump into oncoming traffic. Or leap off the tallest building. Anything than to live this life one more second.

Charles didn't know fate would spare him from this misery. Something incredible happened to Charles on a late afternoon in autumn. His mother tumbled down a flight of stairs while carrying a load of laundry and fractured both knees.

They couldn't afford a doctor's visit. Or medical care. She could no longer provide for the family. The sales traveler's rent covered little. And couldn't be counted on. Charles's mother forced her sons to leave school and work to prevent the apartment from being taken.

His younger brother found work at a brothel down the street. He swept floors and scrubbed stalls after the Johns left. Like his mother did before him. For his labor, he received two native irons every week. Enough to buy a loaf of bread.

Charles fared better. Thirteen native irons a week. A steel mill had hired him on the spot. His job performance was, well, not so great. On Friday, he released a steel bar from the rafters before securing it, and it hit him on the head, knocking him unconscious.

His injury went unnoticed for hours. Until another boy revived him. When he woke, Charles heard voices. One voice introduced itself as God. Sadly, Charles didn't have a direct link to God. He suffered from auditory hallucinations caused by TBI: traumatic brain injury.

The God living inside his head was a hallucination. His limited life experience became his God. Children are great learners. This child's world was limited to a five-mile radius of poverty and violence.

Magistrate Eusebius was born into wealth. He went to the finest institutions in the land. He studied philosophy and religion. He traveled to many lands, near and far. His family owned summer villas in Mountain and River and Valley and Seneca. He dined on purple-footed lynx and tundra caviar and glass-newt most every day. He wore fine silk robes spun from the blunder beetle. Priced at fifty thousand native irons a yard.

A formal education and luxurious travel taught Magistrate Eusebius little in humility. Decency is more to the point. His worldview spanned a five-mile radius, too. Magistrate Eusebius condemned the religious texts for their negative portrayal of God. The God of the ancient text was too barbaric. A genuine monster. No one would ever follow a monster, he had told Dario one night over dinner. As he stuffed his face with purple-footed lynx and sipped fig bubbles.

The pivotal moment spurred him to collaborate with ghostwriters on a rewrite of the ancient text. "This ancient text needs a serious reimagining, a tweak here and there, if you will," he shouted at the team of writers standing by with a finger aimed skyward. "We can do better than God himself, I'm sure of it."

Well, after many rewrites and editorial redevelopments. Endless copy edits and proofreads. Magistrate Eusebius failed. He somehow created, with ghostwriters an earshot away, a more disturbing God than written in the ancient text.

Magistrate Eusebius then decided a boy who could hear the voice of God was more valuable than the ancient texts. Who better to rewrite the word of God than God himself? Fooling with the word of God was one thing. But replacing God had dire consequences. This was a lesson Magistrate Eusebius would never forget.

* * *

"I came as quickly as I could." Charles rushed to Magistrate Eusebius's bedside. The room was mildewy. Dull light from a lamp crawled along the wall. Curtains drawn to erase the daylight clamoring against the windowsill.

It smelled like a dark, undisturbed cave, of which nothing ever escapes. The heart monitor's green laser crept along with a tranquil beep. The tranquil beep took long breaths between. Magistrate Eusebius's heart was slowing down like a dead battery. *It won't be long now before the beeps stop*, Charles thought.

The smell of medication danced in and out. The oxygen machine hummed in the corner as the aroma of plastic and warm machinery crawled up his nose.

Charles inspected Magistrate Eusebius. His bones were frail, as though each limb would shatter under the slightest pressure. That jaundiced skin of his sunk deep, withering beneath the bone.

He tried not to stare for long. Magistrate Eusebius's chest ballooned but didn't move a stitch. Not rising. Not falling. No steady does it. Jutting out like a fairy turtle's back.

Magistrate Eusebius lifted a shaky hand, as though he wanted Charles to kiss it. "My son." The oxygen mask muffled his voice. It sounded like he said *bison*.

Charles removed the mask and held Magistrate Eusebius's hand. "It's done. Your work will live on." After a frail smile, his face quivered under the pressure.

"There's one." Magistrate Eusebius uncontrollably coughed. His body convulsed. Somehow, between the coughs, he managed, "I want their heads."

"Stigmata already deployed the assassin."

Magistrate Eusebius weakly gestured. "Children too." He wore vengeful eyes. "Juliet Saramago, and Julie—" Before he could finish, Magistrate Eusebius pretended to slice his own throat with that skeletal finger.

Charles's eyes spiked like a pulse on a meter. "And Frida Carli—"

Magistrate Eusebius swiped a finger across his throat again. This time, his face looked more sinister than before. "Yes." He grumbled while gritting his teeth. "Everyone."

Like most things in his life, Charles agreed to commit horrific deeds to satisfy. When Charles approved the elimination of everyone on the list, Magistrate Eusebius's face softened like a gentle unicorn.

A raspy tone barreled out. "What?" Magistrate Eusebius coughed in brief intervals. He swallowed hard. But it did him no good. His throat was a box full of needles. "What does our God think—" Magistrate Eusebius's throat seized.

Unbeknownst to Magistrate Eusebius, the voices inside Charles's head were gone. The voice of God had abandoned him nine years, two months, and twenty seconds ago. This was a speculative and preposterous notion, as they did not count days on this planet. Days were irrelevant when the suns rose every six hours. Strangely, not at dawn, as one might surmise. In reality, some people in Mafia Land kept track of the days like they wiped their, well....

Magistrate Eusebius would behead Charles. Like all the others. Had he discovered Charles had been lying to him for nearly a decade. Charles had spoon-fed Magistrate Eusebius political strategies. Not by God's mouth but his. Strategies that advanced his career. Eliminated political rivals. They shouted "Heretic!" at the innocent rivals before beheading them. *Heretic* and *sedition* were the buzzwords of the day.

"Calm yourself, old friend." Charles rested a hand on Magistrate Eusebius's shoulder. "God hears your prayers." Charles didn't believe the words coming out of his mouth. After the voice of God had left, he no longer thought God was real. But it never stopped him from continuing the work that had built a nation. The countless beheadings and hangings. Despite its undeniable cruelty. Now he considered the afterlife a meaningless void.

Magistrate Eusebius tried to raise his trembling hand. "But...but."

Charles lowered his hand and smiled. "God will bless you for doing his work. He will welcome you with open arms."

Magistrate Eusebius shook his head. "I killed so many."

Charles stroked his hair. "Shhh." And gave him a loving look. "I had a wonderful dream last night. God allows me to see the future now."

Magistrate Eusebius wore a serious face. Eager to know the details of Charles's dream.

"I dreamed you were sitting on God's right hand, in the clouds. You were happy and laughing. I never saw such joy come from you."

Magistrate Eusebius's eyes rolled. He let out a heavy breath as though relieving himself. "Someone is standing in." Magistrate Eusebius's shaky finger pointed at the darkest part of the room. Then hit a coughing spell.

Charles whirled around. The dark half of the room was so black he couldn't see a thing. He headed for that dark patch and let his eyes adjust. He stood there for a second, canvasing the space. No one was there. Everything was silent. Except for the machinery humming.

The heart monitor beeped. Then beeped again. Then nothing.

Charles rushed to Magistrate Eusebius's side. Time had passed. Magistrate Eusebius had parted. After seeing the ghost of his father standing in the blackest part of the room. Eyelids half-propped. Mouth agape. His hands twerked, as though strangled to death.

Travelogue

The *blunder beetle* is nocturnal. Mates every fourteen years. And only spins silk between the hours of three and four. Damn those four suns! And so, spends the rest of its time hibernating. To this very day, not a soul has seen the blunder beetle feed. It's a wonder how a creature has lived thousands of years and not eaten a stitch.

Fig bubbles taste nothing like figs—quite the opposite. People cultivate the popular drink from the fool's fig mushroom. People often mistake this mushroom in the wild for fig mushroom because they look the same, hence *fool*. This mushroom has deadly consequences for people who eat it raw. One glass, eight-point-five ounces, will give one hell of a buzz. If one consumes it in copious amounts, this drink will give them the power of the gods and wild hallucinations. Clairvoyants worldwide swear this drink lets them see the future. They say the fool's fig mushroom has a direct link to the universe. Every bottle warns, "Consume at your own risk."

Echo Dimension

PRETTY SOON, the State Department moved from holograms to programmers. They must see it through, all the way. Kill these radical ideas before they even start. Libraries were jam-packed with holograms about how to needlework. Basket weaving. Although, the state's most prized hologram, mailed to every household, was *How to Become a Good Wife*.

Despite their oppressive tendencies, the Land of Kings was an advanced society in terms of technology. They worshipped the digital age. There were downsides. Despite being an advanced society, they still couldn't travel to the stars. Or other planets. In hindsight, they were the opposite of advanced. Since the discovery of electricity, the Land of Kings had no other greater contribution to push society forward.

Every female in the land was suffering from a bad case of anxiety and depression. Take two of these and call me never, because that's the cure to a diseased mind. So they were told by their doctors.

The ease of smuggling literature from the state, paired with ingenuity, delivered the final blow. Using their new knowledge, they crafted a toxic potion. Fatal as venom. The male population's passing was painless. Humane as death can get. Once the compounds entered the bloodstream, within nine seconds, the heart stopped. Ticket punched.

Some of the state leaders had died at the dinner table as supper was being served. Some died seconds after their heads sunk into the pillow. Some died in their favorite recliner while watching the evening news. Some died three at a time. Four at a time, during a rowdy night out with the boys on the I-101.

Most did not mourn their husbands. Some did. Still, that didn't stop them from poisoning their husbands at mealtime. Or whatever time when they spiked their drinks or blabber hoof milk or what have you.

Uncle Stigmata had nailed two things. Girls were far better assassins than boys. Uncle Stigmata put it, "Uneducated assassins were more valuable than gold." Easy to manipulate. They followed orders.

Unbeknownst to Uncle Stigmata, Leonor was a genius. Addy was eager to display her genius. Yet Leonor had learned how to hide it well. Almost impossible to detect.

Uncle Stigmata had received news of Addy's suicide months before Leonor caught wind. He kept Addy's death a secret. When Leonor hadn't heard from Addy in months, she began snooping. And uncovered the truth. Hidden inside the desk drawer of Uncle Stigmata's war room was Addy's death certificate. The Whitehead Academy attached a formal statement to the paperclip. A formal letter written by Salvador, the accountant. It detailed every gory detail. Salvador had written the letter well. In a formal tone. He had worded the letter as if legal advice guided his hand.

Uncle Stigmata had trained Leonor in the ways of the assassin too well. Later that evening, they ate dinner. Had a few laughs. Then went to bed. Never the wiser of Leonor's intention. Leonor wanted him to feel right at home.

When the house settled. Everything was quiet. Except for the sound of an antique clock ticking in the hallway. The hum of vents shuffling warm air into empty spaces. The creaks of a tired house burdened by a hundred years. But still standing.

Leonor slipped out of bed and got to work. She entered Uncle

Stigmata's room light-footed. As though she wore zebra fawn hooves. He didn't even stir in his sleep. She had trained well.

Within minutes, Leonor had bound Uncle Stigmata to the bed. Feet, hands, torso. One could hear a gentle click. The occasional zip of a rope gliding across blunder beetle silk pajamas.

She strapped Uncle Stigmata in tight and straddled his chest. Leonor's weight bearing down on his body startled him. He woke in a frenzy. He tried to flail his arms but couldn't. Uncle Stigmata gasped, as though someone had dunked him in cold water. His eyes were wide and searching, as though his brain couldn't catch up. A deep sleep had him stunned. His voice was faraway, as though he was still dreaming. No longer trusting what his eyes could see. "Leonor?"

Leonor smirked, as though solving an equation. Tilting her head to the right, then left. Her eyes concentrating. Hard at work.

"Leonor?"

She applied an icepick near his eye socket. Uncle Stigmata felt cold steel touching the bridge of his nose. A piercing sting where the point touched his eye canal.

Uncle Stigmata relaxed. Resisted the urge to struggle. Why make a fool of himself? No one could bargain with Leonor. He knew better. He had trained her well. Mercy is not the assassin's way. He closed his eyes and said, "I'm glad it's you, Leonor. Not the Mothers. Now make me proud."

Transorbital lobotomy can be a deadly procedure. It depends on who performs the task. Even for a skilled assassin. Leonor's intentions were not to kill Uncle Stigmata. That would be too easy. "You will live a long life, Uncle. I promise."

Uncle Stigmata looked astounded. He tried to hide his emotions. But nothing inside was in check. Leonor saw fear creeping out. Then relief, as though he could finally breathe again. When she mentioned keeping him alive. "The Mothers will decide."

His relief shifted to shock, then betrayal. His eyes narrowed. Regret spilled forth. "I want you to know something, Leonor. I don't know how you did it, but you crawled inside my heart over the years.

I am not the same man I once was. The Mothers are undeserving of my death. But you are."

"I guess you're right, Uncle." Leonor's eyes darted for a moment, then sharpened. "You betrayed me first."

They say everything happens in time. Perfect time. When time reveals the truth. This was not the first time Uncle Stigmata had betrayed Leonor. He wore a proud face. An assured tone. "My hands were forced. I had no other choice but to kill my brother and your mother. I made a promise to protect you and Addy. Don't you see?" He said this without blinking. "Sometimes you have to do evil things for the good."

Leonor's face shined with an essence of bewilderment. "I was talking about Addy." Her voice quivered. "You didn't tell me Addy died...you...you..." she hadn't stuttered in years. She stuttered when emotions overwhelmed.

Everyone knows or should know when they stumble over the biggest blunder of their life. Uncle Stigmata knew he had just royally fucked up.

Leonor removed the icepick from his eye. "I thought a lobotomy would rage, just like you taught me. Now I think you deserve a harsher punishment." Her eyes watered. Her voice had a faraway tone. "Shh, it's settled."

Switzeeerland & the Accountant

 They were not part of the Mountain region, River, or Valley. No affiliation to the Land of Kings. "I would face beheading before setting up camp with those puny-brained, preposterous men," Salvador often said.

Whitehead sat on the edge of civilization. Surrounded by canyons, rivers, abundant plants, and the ocean. Moist, salty air filled the classrooms every day as it sifted through the blinds. This was an ancient land called Seneca.

Whitehead established his academy to educate the best and brightest. High IQs were acceptable. Though not required. Nor the gold standard. Not the standard one seeks when finding promise. One need only show promise through ingenuity. Whoever pushed the planet forward in any field was the benchmark.

Last year, Whitehead accepted a child named Birgitta who devoted her life to saving the planet. Not just the planet, but to prevent the extinction of human civilization. The year before that, Veda had invented an ordinary device to test deadly chemicals in drinking water.

It mattered little to the individual's social status. Or skin color. Or sex. Or background. Or whatever else. A student needed to show promise. The mission was to find children who could change the world. Not just change it but save it. The greatest minds at Whitehead believed the Land of Kings would eventually annihilate the planet and everyone on it.

On a chilly spring day, the greatest minds at Whitehead came to a depressing conclusion. A mathematical discovery of the ages. Including a hint of doomsday. Space travel would ensure the survival of the species. All species, for that matter. Top mathematicians predicted a catastrophic event would wipe out all life on the planet. Not hypothetical. Guaranteed as death. That analogy they understood. They lived on the fridges of Mafia Land.

From the evidence, Whitehead deduced they must reach the farthest places of the galaxy to ensure survival. As it stood, the world was on its way down, down, down. Terrifyingly quick. Under the status quo, they would never reach space in time. "These primates will blow themselves up and everyone else on the planet," Salvador had muttered too many times.

Life on the planet would also face extinction. At precisely seventy-five years, two months, three days, thirteen minutes, and fifty-three seconds from that chilly spring day. According to an eight-year-old math genius by the name of Emanuel. Who slipped the figures over to Salvador while the meeting got heated.

As noted prior, this figure was hypothetical. Even though time is irrelevant here, the world had to account for some things. Otherwise, no one would ever report for duty. For that matter, the people of Mafia Land would live forever. Mafia Land eternity, that is. "It would be reckless if we didn't." Salvador blurted while eating lavender biscuits and drinking fig bubbles.

Whitehead was betting big on children. They believed future generations were the key. Their minds were fresh and untainted. As untainted as a mind can be in the Land of Kings. But one obstacle loomed. Whitehead wasn't big enough. When you open your doors to the entire world, seating vanishes. Whitehead had a five-year waiting list.

Wealth and gender played a part in educating young people in the

Land of Kings. Gatekeepers alone decided who deserved a proper education.

Poverty-taxed communities had little to no access to a quality education. Through complex political maneuvers, the state stopped providing education funds. Until they paid every native iron in full. Though god doesn't help those who don't pay their taxes.

Whitehead took a different approach. They saw something no one else took notice of. Greatness comes from anywhere. Just like rain falls everywhere on the planet. Through the process of exclusion, which was often the case in these lands. People, or better put, state officials, overlook genius.

Just yesterday, in the poorest region, a child named Amari died from malaria. A curable disease. After his passing, his parents discovered a journal tucked away in a cubby.

Every day for two years, Amari painstakingly recorded all his knowledge in the journal. While tinkering with an engine in his dad's garage, Amari had had a breakthrough. An ah-ha moment while playing with greasy pistons and gears.

Amari had noticed how certain machine lubricants interacted with light. His father had a plethora of oil lying about in the garage. Gear oil. Motor oil. Piston oil. Spark-plug oil. Battery oil. He began testing the elasticity and glittery molecules by holding them to the light.

What his parents didn't know was that Amari was obsessed with oil. Its properties mystified. He spent days jotting down ideas on how to manipulate oil. All because of machines. He stumbled into advancements in quantum computing. Quantum computer chips, in particular. His discovery was greater than the invention of electricity. Nobody had a clue how groundbreaking this was. Not even Amari.

He discovered workarounds to cool a quantum processor through highly refined silicon. Laid out in a pattern of dots. Quantum computers need good airflow and lubrication to avoid overheating. Like an engine. Thus, preventing blowing the fuck up in someone's face.

In any event, his parents had difficulty transcribing Amari's journal. His father was an auto mechanic. His mother, a schoolteacher.

Luckily, his mother recognized its importance. When they didn't know what to make of the journal, they decided the best course of action was to ship it off to Whitehead for further analysis. From there, silicon dots made quantum computing a household name.

* * *

"Chancellor Dario." Salvador rested his elbows on the desk, fingers laced in a triangle. "I evaluated your nephew's test. He didn't place in any category."

Chancellor Dario flailed his hand, as though shooing a panda bee. "I've always admired your game play, Salvador. That's why I'm prepared to double my offer."

Salvador sat there, eyes piercing straight ahead. Lips narrowed. "It's not a question of money."

"How much?"

"No amount. If I allow your nephew to skate the rules, then I'd have to say yes to every state child. Every wealthy merchant in the land, for that matter. I must respectfully decline."

Chancellor Dario pointed a jaundiced finger at Salvador. "If you don't allow my nephew to attend Whitehead, then I'll withdraw my holdings."

Chancellor Dario's threat didn't shock Salvador. He almost seemed amused by that snarky grin. "Be very mindful. You may not like—"

"Now."

"There is one thing we must discuss."

Chancellor Dario moved to interrupt Salvador. Yet Salvador flashed his palm. "I will transfer your holdings in no less than thirty seconds. But once the process is complete, there's no going back. Your money will no longer carry Whitehead protection. The state, or any other region, could rob you blind." Salvador took a sip of platinum elixir and set the glass on the desk.

Chancellor Dario formed razor eyes and hiked his arms. He clearly had no intentions of responding.

Salvador stared back, got bored, and looked at his watch as if he were late for an appointment. "Would you like to proceed?"

Chancellor Dario sprung to his feet. "You allowed Addy Ferrante to attend. Why not do the same for my nephew?"

Salvador wore a puzzled expression and thought for a few seconds. "Adelaide Ferrante is a genius." He lowered his hands and laid them flat on the desk. "Your nephew is confrontational and abusive. He was disruptive during the test. He then argued with the instructor. When the instructor requested he take his seat, he got into his face. We take that sort of behavior very seriously at Whitehead."

"Bullshit!"

"If I may continue." Salvador peered at Chancellor Dario like a bug he could pop at any moment. "I rarely say this, but your nephew is not Whitehead material. I wouldn't allow him to attend this school for all the money in the world."

Chancellor Dario readied himself to storm out the door when Salvador stopped him. "Chancellor, I'd like to clear the air before you rush off."

Chancellor turned, still wearing vengeful eyes. "Our business will continue as planned."

"No, that's not what I'm referring to. I was unaware of your affiliation with the Ferrante family."

Chancellor Dario wore a guilty face. He refused to make eye contact and glued his eyes to the floor, trying his best to avoid Salvador's tractor beams. "There's no affiliation."

Salvador held up a finger, as if lecturing. "You called her Addy as though you know the girl."

"And?"

"It's a simple question, Chancellor."

"I don't have time for your silly games, Salvador."

Chancellor Dario stormed out of the office, slamming the door behind. Walls shook, pictures on the walls jittered, and Chancellor Dario never answered the question.

* * *

Often, it matters little what land one lives. Land of Kings or any other region is a quark planet at heart. The place one lives is astronomical when everything in life goes sunny side up.

There's nothing like feeling swallowed up, when the world tumbles down a black hole. When things go up in smoke, the world is quark sized. Filled with bizarre coincidence. Bizarre turns of events.

Before Addy did what she did, she wrote a letter addressed to Fernando Saramago. One would think there couldn't be two Fernando Saramagos running wild in this disgraceful land. Under normal circumstances, most would agree. But, to clarify, two Fernando Saramagos were very much alive and well. They lived in the same providence. One point two miles and some change away from each other. One lived in a modest house on an instructor's salary. And the other a castle. State salary. The one who lived in a modest house was brother to the future Mother Saramago. The one who lived in the castle was Chancellor Dario's brother.

Chancellor Dario's Fernando had relations with Addy. Mother Saramago's Fernando was guilty of teaching Addy. Nothing more. Following Addy's suicide, Fernando's accusations burdened Tetchy's mother. Which later, she found out, he never did.

He had declared his innocence many times. Even right before his death. No matter how desperately he tried to convince others. Drawing back to his flawless reputation. Pointing out again and again that his spotless record was solid gold. Nothing he said would suffice. Nothing he did would suffice. He passed three lie detectors, then the mood changes. Not only was he a child abuser, but now he was a cold, calculated criminal who could fool a lie detector.

Fernando Saramago did everything in his power to prove his innocence. He underwent DNA testing. Hair samples collected from both heads. Semen. He surrendered all his personal devices to the state. His life was an open book, he told one investigator. Whatever it took to clear his name. He cooperated beyond what a guilty person would dare.

In nine days, they found no evidence that Fernando Saramago had had relations with Addy. No surveillance footage. No texts. No correspondents of any kind. His DNA didn't match. The investigation grew wild by the miles. A hundred in the opposite direction.

They interviewed all the instructors at Whitehead. One by one, they tumbled down the baba foot hole. Then, the entire staff. Even the custodians. Especially the ones who worked late at night. Then the children. Every single one. One by one. Days and days. Hour upon hour. Minute after minute. But they had no leads. No particular direction in which to go.

"Surely," the lead investigator claimed, "more victims will come forward. His colleagues must have seen something. Known something. How could they not?"

But the investigation stalled. Every person they interviewed adored Fernando Saramago. The students raved about him. His colleges attested to his gifted abilities. Even the custodians adored him. Everyone at Whitehead loved him.

Jessica Hart, a freshman who had received her first D by Mr. Saramago, said during her interview, "Mr. Saramago gave me a D—a D! It was bullshit. He said I wasn't pushing myself hard enough. My creativity lacked. Lacked," she repeated for emphasis, slapping her forehead.

"Tell us more," the lead investigator said, as though he could almost taste Fernando Saramago's blood splash in his mouth. Jessica Hart was the first person they had run across that had dirt on Fernando Saramago. Tingles radiated to the back of his head. "Don't leave out a single thing. Even the stuff that doesn't seem important. Because you never know. It might be just the thing we're looking for."

Jessica Hart changed her tone in the middle of his pathetic plea. "He was right. I wasn't pushing myself hard enough." She was almost in tears now. "Because of him, now I write the best stuff of my life." She then bawled.

Considering the evidence. Or lack thereof. The lead investigator came to a very disturbing conclusion. Fernando Saramago's background was too squeaky-clean. As if someone had scrubbed it from the dark web. Fernando Saramago was now a mastermind who cohorted with seditious types. The lead investigator claimed

Fernando Saramago was living a double life. No evidence to support such a conclusion, just a hunch.

Fernando Saramago must have had burner phones and laptops hidden in the walls. Or a secret lair to perform all his perverted acts.

Fernando, with a heavy heart, realized something no one else did. The investigation would never end. On day three, after interviewing with the lead investigator, something deep inside gave a whisper. The lead investigator would pursue the case relentlessly. Until Fernando was executed for a crime, he didn't commit.

The lead investigator's demeanor revealed it all. The way he spoke. That miserable, haunting glare that kept beating Fernando into submission. Fernando clearly saw the investigation was heading one way. The lead investigator wanted to bathe in his blood. He wouldn't stop until he did.

On day nine, the lead investigator served a warrant to tear apart the modest home. The one he had scrimped and saved for his entire life. To save his son and wife from further shame. Embarrassment speaks more to the truth. He did what he had to. In his mind, the only person who could end the madness was Fernando. He hoped that, years from now, his innocence would be revealed. He yearned for vindication. Long after his soul had departed from this land.

***

Adelaide Ferrante was a sneak and boy crazy. She was a Heather. Yet the students often overlooked her beauty. Her presence intimidated the boys. Some even called her a freak as she bumped shoulders in the hall, after the bell rang.

She was part of a select group. In truth, Addy was far more exceptional than any student at Whitehead. Only two hundred people in the world had scored higher than two hundred on an IQ. Addy was one of them. Which was rare indeed. Though her social net worth ranked south of zero and was heading toward double negative territory.

In some circles, gifted people should avoid the public at all costs. Profoundly gifted people are freaks of nature. Lacking social grace.

Temperamental. Not empathetic. And live on another planet. All according to Chancellor Dario's dossier. Which, for once in his miserable life, he hit that one on the nose. This was the case. In Addy's case.

People always welcome honesty. But the delivery method matters. And who delivers it. Addy was a little too honest and pushy and temperamental and high-strung.

Enzo, a sophomore who thought Addy was attractive, blurted, "I'd like to bounce that ass." as she passed them in the hall.

She then paused, and repeated something she had overheard him say to Hugo, another sophomore. "How about I bounce *your* ass?"

Even though she had inserted herself into a private conversation. The delivery of her tone sounded threatening. Yes, she was a noob. Despite her threatening delivery. Addy was ready to mix it up with Enzo. In a good, nonthreatening sort of way. Though Enzo and Hugo didn't take it that way.

Enzo looked shook. Hugo wore a confused expression. Almost analyzing with his eyes how bouncing his ass would all work out. Enzo shook his head. "No, I'm good. For real." Then the two boys scattered quick.

Whitehead Academy sat nestled in Seneca Township, a futuristic city. Skyscrapers made of bio-cladding. Self-healing streets. 3-D mycelium lampposts. Superstrong plastic. Tougher than steel. Dubbed 2DPA-1. Immersive technology flooded venues. Crystal solar bikes. Everything powered by the four suns. Super bionic surveillance kept crime levels low. For Mafia Land standards, or course.

Despite the rule forbidding Whitehead students from leaving campus. Addy went outside the laser gates, anyway. While in her dorm, she saw Pierre Durand, the groundskeeper, sneak past the gate. Somewhere between the brick wall and laser gate was a small opening. She slipped out most every day. At six sharp. Right after Peirre Durand made his grand escape.

Addy had plenty of funds. Uncle Stigmata was generous. Excessively, from a financial perspective. For a teenage girl. Never giving it a second thought about where Addy would spend all that dough.

Smart Cafés, hologram centers, virtual libraries, fine dining, interested her little. Even the greatest geniuses are not immune to human tendencies. Or better. The human desire for needs and wants. Know this: the world hides seedy places where the bored can disappear. People say intelligent people succumb to boredom. Maybe explaining Addy's case. Except she got more than she had bargained for.

At the tail end of summer, she met Chancellor Dario's Fernando at a rager downtown. Fernando and Addy, and a little nudge from Molly, danced all night until closing time.

After their second date, when Fernando introduced himself. Once the Molly wore off. Addy thought their chance encounter was fate. She was not only crushing all over him, but she also thought she was in love. Dog-eared inside her head for eternity was Fernando Saramago. Chancellor Dario's Fernando was as basic as it got. As basic as Sebastian Carlito. No relation. But if one knew no better…

Needs are a funny beast. Add trauma to the mix. When faced with trauma, healthy needs collapse to fumes. Eager to hold the hand of anyone who will listen. Anyone who will fill in those basic needs. Life sometimes reveals the disastrous consequences of obsession.

Chancellor Dario's Fernando was far from a daddy. He was a hunch back with pencil legs that reached to his neck. Not a stitch of hair on his head. Baby hands that smelled of hard-boiled baba foot eggs.

Birthright alone forgave all. Despite his physical limitations, he excelled in other parts. For example, evil crafted his tongue from zigzag silk. His lies were not delectable. Exceptionally good as good can get when corrupting young, naive minds. He had Addy wrapped the moment he opened his mouth. Every word he spilled was a fairytale. He knew what to say and how to say it.

* * *

"There was an ancient land that lived on this very soil before Seneca," Charles said while slamming the last drop of elixir in his cup. "I believe you Senecans called it Switz End. Did I pronounce that part right?"

101

"No." Salvador rolled his eyes with a face full of disgust. "It's pronounced Switzeeerland. Switzerland." Repeating himself in the hopes the word would dig into Charles's brain.

"Well," Charles flicked his hand, "you knew what I meant."

Salvador removed one of the color coded glass tablets from the towering shelf behind. "How do you keep track of the world's wealth inside a hologram tablet?" Charles crossed his leg. "I mean, with all this technology laying around, you'd think the information would be safer inside of a virtual program."

Salvador scoffed. Waved his hand over his head. Ignoring his comment as though Charles were an annoying insect buzzing around. "Hackers cannot hack holograms, now can they?"

"I suppose you're right." Charles switched legs. He raised his finger to the ceiling. "But they can *steal* it."

"Yes, yes." Salvador was growing more agitated by the second. "It would do them little good. They'd have to decipher the contents first. I'm the only one with the encryption," he said, finger tapping his temple where a glass square blinked.

Charles jeered and straightened his pant leg. The cuff of his slacks rode high, revealing his bright socks against a black wool fabric. "A programmer could dissect a hologram in seconds."

Salvador stopped what he was doing and gave Charles a dead-eye and tossed the glass tablet. It landed at the edge of the desk. Tittering with a loud tink. Salvador flailed his hands. "Please, by all means. I'm confident your programmers would fail miserably."

Charles waved his hand, gesturing a surrender. "Salvador." He squirmed in his chair. "That's not what I meant. It's just, it's a lot of money."

"Numbers, Charles." Salvador raised his hands. "They're only numbers to connect commodities. These things don't have a heart. A soul." Salvador pointed at his temple. "They have no value when you're sick or dying. Gold won't cure death."

"Oh, come now, Salvador." Charles was now perched at the edge of his seat. "What else would people do if they had nothing to work toward? To build something useful beyond their miserable, insignificant lives. They wouldn't know how to spend their time wisely without those imaginary things to keep them going."

"Aw, yes." Salvador rolled his eyes again. "These imaginary things have reduced the world's IQ. No one reads anymore, Charles. They rather buy a hologram to sum up the story. Or spend their days in a virtual world. They don't think for themselves anymore." He fluttered his fingers.

"There's no winning with you, Salvador." Charles leaned back, folding his hands in his lap. "I'd like to discuss Chancellor Dario's unique situation, if I may be so bold."

"The answer is still no," Salvador said and pointed to the ground. "His nephew will never set foot in this institution."

Charles shook his head. "No, it's not about him. His nephew is a bit of a pecker. It's something much more serious than that."

Salvador straightened his posture and perched at the edge of his seat. Brows scrunched and arms folded on the desk. "I don't scare easily, Charles, yet you did just that."

"Fernando Saramago has developed an expensive drug habit. He owes all the ragers in town quite a bit of money."

Salvador's eyes rose high, his mouth slack. "Instructor Fernando Saramago?" His voice was high-pitched. A tone Salvador seldom used.

Charles looks bewildered. "I suppose we have two Fernando Saramagos."

Salvador didn't respond, still wearing a shocked expression, and anxiously waited for Charles to elaborate.

"Chancellor Dario has a brother named Fernando Saramago."

"I was unaware Chancellor Dario had blood ties to the Saramagos."

"He doesn't." Charles's curt tone radiated. "They stole the name to gain political favor with the state. You know as well as I, the Saramago name still holds power in certain circles. People are still sentimental about ancient names."

Salvador shrugged and scratched his head. "My time is valuable, Charles. Get to the point."

"Fernando Saramago had relations with Adelaide Ferrante."

War the Witch's Brew

WAR WEARS MANY FACES. Some delight in it. Are masters of it. Others run in the face of it. In the opposite direction, doing light speed in a twenty, like a zigzag. Or however quick the feet can carry them toward safety. Some find themselves thrust into it. And have no other choice but to fight their way out. Some don't even know war has landed on their doorstep. Not until someone delivers a death note by mistake. Forwarding address, if you please.

War had landed on the Mothers' doorstep. More like the Valley Region Fitness Center's doorstep. At noon. On the dot. An Amazon courier had left a box at the front desk. Where children and women checked in and out for their daily robust fix.

A woman of twenty-three, who went by the name Sofia, omitted a last name upon registration. Later, the Mothers would uncover the mysterious woman's true identity. Though they thought nothing of it. Women learned to live in the shadows those days.

A woman, especially younger, rarely left the house without a chaperone. Most women lived a double life. Not by choice. They guarded their anonymity as though life or death hung in the balance. And it most certainly did. One tiny mistake was all it took. Talking to the wrong person. Wrong place, wrong time. Spilling too much information could get a woman hung in the square. Where children and mothers tried not to look up at those foreign agents hanging as they went about their day in the busy square.

Elizabeth Marquez ran the front of the house at the fitness center. She was the first person to open the death note. The Mothers had never seen a death note before. This caused a chain of bloody events. The thing that broke the blabber hoof's back. To move forward, sometimes backward, is the order that makes sense.

Months before, Sofia had come to the center to soak in the hot tub. Nobody had recognized her. Nobody had ever seen her before. Not even around town. She was a ghost bride.

Elizabeth noticed Sofia hobbling her way toward the front desk. Nursing that left leg. Her face told the story. The face can't keep its big mouth shut. She winced and gritted her teeth with every step. Determined to reach her destination. Neither made a sound nor moaned in pain.

Her skin was youthful and flawless. Her clothes were neat and clean. Hair tidy. Nails manicured. Yet a lifetime of torment marred her face. Sadness, perhaps. Something not so easy to place. Something eerie simmered beneath the surface of those eyes, Elizabeth later noted.

"Sprain an ankle, did we?"

Sofia seemed ashamed by the question. She forced a smile. Kept eyes glued to the floor. "I'm such a klutz."

Klutz? Elizabeth shook her head. For the first time in a while, she softened her tone. "The hot tub is a trek. I'll get you a wheelchair."

"I can make it."

Elizabeth walked around to the other side of the counter. "It's no trouble, girl. Besides, they keep me cooped up behind this thing all day."

Sofia's face turned red. Her eyes filled with panic. Hands trembling, she said, "I'm fine, really."

"I insist."

The two settled near the hot tub. Under better lighting. Sofia's thigh was dark purple, as though squeezed to death by a vice. The first word that came to Elizabeth was *torture*. Someone had tortured the young woman. She had seen these marks before on other women. By whom, though, is what Elizabeth wanted to know.

She helped Sophia mount two small steps and sunk her into the heated water. Plunging into the hot tub produced a puckered face. Squinty eyes and lips locked tight. She started breathing hard and groaned.

"Don't fight it. The hard part is over." Sofia couldn't get a look at Elizabeth's expression. But she, too, mirrored the pain. Her face crumpled in agony. "Do you live alone?"

"Tomorrow is our anniversary."

"Children?"

Sofia didn't respond. Instead, she wore a sad face with glazed-over eyes. The air was warm and thick. The sharp scent of chlorine burned the nose and eyes and made the inside of her nostrils itch. Elizabeth held her nose, an attempt to taper a sneeze. "Someday, perhaps."

"I hope not." Sofia lowered her head. "Does that make me a bad person? I mean, to not want children? Women are supposed to want children." Her voice echoed against the porcelain tile as if they were in a tunnel. The pool area had floor-to-ceiling tile.

"No." Elizabeth rubbed her nose as though she were about to sneeze. The chlorine made her teary-eyed. Even though the jets weren't purring. The water in the tub was calm. Elizabeth hadn't turned on the motor yet. "It's your body. I didn't want children either when I was…" Elizabeth stopped herself from explaining further.

"Do you?" Sophia turned to look at her. Eyes pained. "Have children, I mean."

"One." Elizabeth's face illuminated for a second. Watery eyes. Not sure if she was teary-eyed because of the chlorine or Sofia's mangled leg. "Juliette."

"What changed your mind?"

"Love."

When Elizabeth mentioned love, Sofia's eyes flashed with envy and flickered far away, as though the power of her eyes could take her from that place. "I'll never know, love."

* * *

A week had gone by, and Sofia had not returned to the fitness center. Elizabeth feared the worst and agonized over the idea that she may never see Sofia again.

Still, and foremost, she didn't lose hope. She stayed behind that counter, watching every person who entered. But none were Sofia. The young woman who wore plain threads. Something you'd pick up from a bargain store. Not clothes of poverty, rather necessity.

Elizabeth about gave up hope when Sofia hobbled into the fitness center on a Monday. Her limp was worse than before. On that sweltering day, Sofia wore a long-sleeved turtleneck.

Elizabeth almost didn't recognize her. She snatched a wheelchair and wheeled Sofia to the hot tub. Not until Sofia undressed did Elizabeth's heart grow mighty homicidal. Her blood raced and heart stung, as though a knife had pierced through all that chlorine vapor.

Sofia seemed infected by something that almost blackened her leg and traveled to the right side. Handprints bruised her neck. Elizabeth rubbed her neck as though someone had choked her. Torture entered her mind again. *That husband of hers won't stop until she's dead.*

Elizabeth could almost feel those invisible hands choking her. Squeezing the life from her. "He'll never stop. No matter how many times he promises." Shocked by her own admission. Her lack of control to keep her mouth shut. She stared at the back of Sofia's head, waiting for her to say something, anything.

Seconds slowed, and Sofia didn't respond. Elizabeth wasn't afraid to speak her mind anymore. Sofia had freed her. Freed her from the weight of oppression. Elizabeth no longer cared if the state hung her in the square beside the others for speaking out.

Somewhere deep down, she thought this might be her last chance to save the young woman. She could feel it in her bones. "Leave him before it's too late." She almost screamed as though her words could kill the husband.

Sofia held the silence. She stared straight ahead, as though she had accepted her fate. Whatever that may be. However long that may be. A king's hand she'd die under. That was her fate. No one could stop that. No one.

"I can protect you. My husband isn't a state sympathizer. We own a vacation house in the countryside. No one will know where to look."

Before Elizabeth could hatch a rescue plan, Sofia turned around. "He always finds me. If he finds out who helped me, he'll kill you first, then your daughter." Her eyes, full of terror, told the story. Sofia said this, but she didn't seem convinced by her own words.

"Who is this man who does these horrible things to you?"

Sofia used a tone that implied, isn't it obvious? "Dario." No need to explain further. Elizabeth didn't wear an ounce of surprise. "Chancellor Dario." Of course. By all appearances, his handiwork exceeded him. He was, rumor had it, sadistic. She thought Sofia had married a simple man because she wore plain threads. Her gaze remained fixed on the suburbs, not a castle. Sofia didn't exude a regal demeanor befitting a chancellor's wife like all the others. Not by appearance. Not by anything. Not a stitch of wealth dwelled within those bones. Then again, Chancellor Dario was a monster.

Sofia reached out her hand. "I don't enjoy asking for help, but I don't think I can climb out."

Elizabeth helped Sofia dress. That's when Elizabeth got a good, hard look at Chancellor Dario's cruelty. During that intimate moment, clarity emerged. Elizabeth had decided.

Before Sofia left the fitness center, Elizabeth made a last attempt. "I brewed some wonderful tea," she said so sugary. "I insist you have some with me before you leave."

At first, Sophia seemed hesitant. Though Elizabeth was wearing those kind eyes. Eyes you couldn't say no to. "I have to be back at one. Not a second longer."

They sat. Sofia swirled the spoon in the cup. The spoon screeching the porcelain radiated a pathetic cry. Then she winced as she placed it on a napkin. The spoon left wet dimples on the tissue. She took a small sip. The liquid was warm. Notes of whipper sweets. The color of amber. Vapor rose from the cup like morning mist. The taste of juniper coating her tongue. "You haven't touched your cup."

"It's too late in the day. This one's for you."

The tea's flavor captivated her instantly. The first sip seemed to calm her nerves. Almost sedative, as though she didn't give a shit about anything anymore. Especially Dario. She kept sipping away because the tea was so tasty. And grew tastier by the second and popped with exotic flavors. And the more she drank, the more her surroundings grew brighter. Suddenly, she felt joyous. Giddy even. She started laughing. Why the hell was she laughing? It felt so good to laugh again because she hadn't laughed in years.

A slight problem existed. She always vibe-checked her surroundings. She never let her guard down. No matter what. Except this time. Elizabeth wasn't laughing. Elizabeth looked serious. Almost heartbroken. Sofia began playing with Elizabeth's lips, moving them up and down. "Don't be so angry," Sofia said. "Everything will be fine."

Sofia continued to laugh and use that low baritone as though she were drunk. "That should do it." Elizabeth reached for Sofia's cup, but she yanked it back.

"Hey, that's my tea." Sofia pointed at Elizabeth's cup. "That's your cup, and this is mine. For once in my life, I'd like my own darn cup. Okay?"

"Everyone deserves their own cup."

"Exactly." Sofia said, pointing a finger at Elizabeth.

"I think that's plenty. Give it here."

"Fuck Dario." She measured something invisible with her fingers. "He's this tiny. Did I ever tell you that?"

Elizabeth's demeanor shifted. She wore the devil's face with a slight grin. "You won't have to fear him anymore because I plan to cut off his fucking head."

Sofia's eyes shot up. She was speechless for a second. A serious look about her. "You can't say stuff like that. It's dangerous." Sofia's eyes went delirious. "Don't you dare let them take me. Promise me you won't let them take me."

"Mark my words."

Sofia smiled, showing all her teeth, even the back ones. Then, without warning, Sofia's forehead crashed into the table. Wham. Lights out. The cup spun off the table and shattered on the floor.

The sound of fine porcelain shattering reverberated. Elizabeth nervously looked about the room, praying no one saw the chancellor's wife slam that pretty little face into the table.

She waited to see if Sofia would reanimate. Elizabeth knew some reanimated after drinking the tea. Some never woke, depending on how much they consumed. She didn't intend to kill Sofia, but to drug her and take her some place safe. Far away from Dario.

Elizabeth checked Sofia's pulse. It was throbbing a little too fast, yet steady. Her biggest concern was that Sofia's wrist had turned cold. Before Elizabeth could retrieve the wheelchair and load Sofia, a man entered the leisure room. He wore an impeccable suit. Hair slicked. Not a strand out of place. The man looked Dario bougie. But thuggy in one swoop. It was those menacing, dark eyes that gave it away. They seemed to exaggerate the man into a goblin smack.

"Yes, what is it? You have no right being here." Elizabeth knew better than to talk to a man that way. Who was she?

He gave her a frightful look that gave her the heebie-jeebies. The man pointed at Sofia. "I'm the chancellor's driver."

Elizabeth stumbled over her words. "She's...she's not well." She looked around for something sharp. Anything to put him down fast without drawing attention. "Wait outside, and I'll wheel her out to the car."

"No." He folded his massive arms with those menacing eyes sharpened like daggers. "She comes with me now."

Elizabeth kept searching for something to grab. Something to knock this guy sideways. "If you don't leave."

"What?" He edged closer.

Elizabeth flinched.

"That's right, you'll do nothing."

In her head, Sofia's last words played: "Promise me you won't let them take me." Elizabeth had made Sofia a promise. And she wouldn't let her down. With nothing left to lose, Elizabeth screamed a horrifying scream.

Cristina sprinted into the leisure room full of panic. Then Gabriella joined. The sight of a man was all they needed to know. "You're not allowed here," Cristina said.

"I'm the chancellor's driver. I'm here to retrieve his wife."

Retrieve, Gabriella thought. *What is she, an animal?* "Clearly she can't defend herself from the likes of you, and we have no intentions."

He lunged forward and raised his hand like he would smack the hell out of her.

All three jumped back.

Cristina pointed a damning finger. "That will be the biggest mistake of your life."

* * *

In the end, they had no power to protect Sofia. Not when it involved a chancellor's wife. The man loaded Sofia's body into the flying limo and flew off.

They had a strict set of rules concerning the tea. Cristina worried that their little secret would garner the attention of the state. The deep state. But, more importantly, that it might fall into the wrong hands. A rare alkaloid, dwarf-seed extract, formed the base of the tea. Which sedated five to ten hours, give or take. Concentrated amounts could kill a goblin smack in seconds.

What began as experimental, such as giving your husband a sleeping cocktail, changed their trajectory. They soon realized tainted batches could kill. The three of them found a workaround in their current position in life. A few sips was all it took. Then lights out. "You better hope the chancellor doesn't find out what we've created."

"I hope he does. I really do." Elizabeth was sweeping shards of porcelain into a dustpan. "I'm tired of playing these games. I just hope he doesn't kill her before he finds out the truth."

* * *

The next day, at four sharp, Elizabeth sat at the counter and prayed Sofia would walk through those double doors. But she never did. Instead, a package arrived seconds after four. Addressed to Diego and Alina Fuentes. Which, sometime later, Elizabeth would discover were Sofia's parents. Upon further inspection, Elizabeth saw in bold letters:

SHIP TO:

Diego Fuentes/ Alina Fuentes

4913 17th Avenue

Valley, Mafia Land

Curious to know what was inside, Elizabeth ripped open the Amazon package. And what did she see? There's a moment in everyone's life when a situation obliterates the soul and plunges them into darkness for good. And, on this day, Elizabeth's soul sank into an endless, dark well. And would never return to the light of day.

When she peered down at Sofia's lifeless eyes resting inside that godless, gold-lined tissue box. Everything inside herself shattered like that fucking porcelain cup. Sedition pervaded. In reality, the biggest one that stood out to Elizabeth was the hint of juniper that wafted upward.

In her last days, Sofia had updated her parents' address at the last second and forward all their mail to the fitness center. Nobody knew why. But some in Mafia Land claimed this pivotal moment in history had ignited the long war. War must have been unavoidable and written in the stars when freedom was at stake.

Five days later, someone made an announcement on social media. Chancellor Dario had wed another young woman. She had just turned eighteen. Right before Chancellor Dario made the announcement. And who do you suppose he wed on that fateful day? None other than Lucia Fuentes, Sofia's baby sister. They looked identical. The only difference—one had blue eyes, the other a lush forest.

Some hope still existed. Elizabeth stuck to her promise. What the three women realized, after much deliberation and horror. Women had been fighting a losing battle for centuries in the Land of Kings. Women and girls spent their days praying men would change their ways. And more to the point, that men would create a law granting equal rights to everyone in the land. But they never did. Days before the long war began, authorities prevented the female population from leaving the house unless chaperoned. They had been fooling themselves, thinking it would go any other way but a trail of blood.

Elizabeth stuck to her word in the literal sense. She cut off Chancellor Dario's head. And mailed it to the State Department in a gold-tissue-lined box.

Sometimes going back two spaces is the only way forward. She didn't stop there. Dario had an older brother who, according to an informant at the State Department, aided in the torture and mutilation of Sofia.

So, Elizabeth pickled his head too and started delivering her own death notes of many to come. She shipped his head to their mother, Angelia Montoya. Then, after that, Miguel Montoya, Angelia's husband, for insurance. One can never be too certain which bush the raspberries fall from.

Travelogue

The *death note* was not the Mothers' invention. Chancellor Dario had invented the barbaric practice. He pickled his wife's head and wrapped it in gold tissue paper and doused the box in juniper. His wife's favorite perfume. The one she wore when they had first met. Way before Dario was chancellor.

Potions, Mayhem & a Lock of Hair

DEADLY POTIONS WERE ideal when handling political affairs. High-profile assassinations were sensitive matters. That required the utmost discretion. Uncle Stigmata introduced Leonor to the deadly art of potion making. "There are two ways to eliminate a target." Uncle Stigmata's voice pierced the silence while Leonor sat in a chair. Hanging on every word. "First," he raised a finger, "poison."

Disappointment shone on her face.

"I know. I know. Not a thrilling way to hone your combat kills." He raised another finger with excitement. "A true assassin must sometimes ever so quietly eliminate the target. Preferably in their sleep. So as not to arouse suspicion. I call this the intimate kill."

Leonor nodded and perked up. All bright eyed and perched at the edge of her seat.

"The second is to get your hands dirty. The messier, the better. You're not baking cakes. Or sending well wishes. You're there to murder another human being. A true assassin must bathe in their target's blood. If they want to send the right message. As I'm sure you do."

Leonor hiked her hand. "Uncle Stigmata, how does a true assassin know when to poison or get dirty?"

Uncle Stigmata paused, embroiled in thought. "If there was a pop quiz, Leonor, you'd surely fail. A true assassin would never ask such foolish questions. I will not think for you. It's instinct. It's a feeling in the pit of your gut." He slapped his stomach for dramatic effect. "You can't teach instincts. The kill must pump through every vein in your body." He tapped his temple so hard it thunked. "You should be able to read my mind when I hand you a burn notice." He slumped into a seat. "From the start, I showed you how to take emotions out of the equation. That only applies when you're slicing someone's throat. A guilty conscience is a death sentence."

Uncle Stigmata swigged fig bubbles from a blue jade goblet. Then wiped his lips clean. "This is a unique feeling. A true assassin must know when to apply either method. Yes, sometimes one must apply both. I've seen it before under rare circumstances. Now." He dug into his vest pocket and yanked out a small vial and held it to the light. He cradled it, forefinger to thumb, as though the vial might bite. "This is an odorless, tasteless potion. I call it Sabrina-32, named after the inventor's daughter, plagued by insomnia."

He placed the vial in Leonor's palm. "You must carry Sabrina-32 with you. Consider it part of an assassin's uniform."

Leonor mimicked Uncle Stigmata and held it to the light. The liquid inside was clear. She was astonished by the vial's size. "How does it work?" Her voice was full of wonder.

"What do you mean?" Uncle Stigmata gasped. Almost choking on fig bubbles. "Have you gone deaf all the sudden? It quietly eliminates the target." He took an angry swig of fig bubbles. Side-eyeing her.

She rolled her eyes. "I get that. What I mean is, how do I use it?"

He gave Leonor a serious look and pointed at the vial dangling from her fingertips. "You must be very careful when handling Sabrina-32. The skin easily absorbs its compounds. One drop will knock you out for twelve hours. Give or take. But two drops will stop your heart instantly. No coming back from that one." He giggled and swigged more fig bubbles.

"So I could slip it into your drink, and you'd never know?"

Uncle Stigmata sets down his goblet and stopped giggling.

* * *

Uncle Stigmata made the fatal mistake of admitting he had murdered Leonor's parents. Leonor was going to make him pay for those transgressions and for Addy. Addy's blood was on his hands.

Her parents would have never allowed Addy to attend Whitehead. It also raised a serious question: If her parents were still alive, would she have become an assassin?

Even though she didn't mind the killing part. She enjoyed escaping consequences. Sneaking around a target's home without getting caught. The power to decide one's fate gave her a rush. As though she had drunk a gallon of zinger blood. She, in a strange sense, played god.

Leonor dangled Sabrina-32 in his face.

"Oh, bless you, child." Uncle Stigmata was relieved. "You care for me, after all. I always wondered about that. I was rather fond of you."

She wagged her finger. "You should have listened to that gut feeling, Uncle. Because I was going to kill you, eventually. Way before this." That sinister tone steamed up his face. "One drop should do it." Leonor stretched out her finger. "On second thought, maybe half a drop. We want you nice and lively."

What Uncle Stigmata didn't realize was that Leonor had been experimenting with the side effects of Sabrina-32. She had tweaked the formula. Adding a dash of this and that. Creating something that had razor teeth. She wanted Sabrina-32 to grow hairy legs and deadly venom.

He tried to move his head, but it wouldn't budge. She had strapped his limbs down tight, including his head. She drew a tiny amount of Sabrina-32 with a pipette. She rested her hand near his eye. "Be very still. We don't want to stop the heart."

Uncle Stigmata angrily wiggled. Then shouted obscenities. But surrendered at once. Deep down, he knew he couldn't reason with Leonor. He had trained her well. He accepted his fate. "I regret nothing. I did what I did for the Land of Kings." He wiggled his arm. Gesturing a pathetic, invisible salute for gold, god, and glory.

His words meant little. Leonor expected less. Much less. She squeezed a tiny drop of liquid into his eye. Once the liquid coated the cornea, he blinked a few times. "You lack imagination. I didn't feel a thing."

Leonor smiled. Confident in her ability to update Sabrina-32 to this century. Sabrina-32-2.0 raced through his veins. Quicker than the words tumbling out of his mouth. He didn't have time to react. Then passed out.

* * *

Leonor was a talented snoop. A thorough snoop. She uncovered two important details while rummaging through Uncle Stigmata's study. Addy's death certificate. And a kill list. A kill list Uncle Stigmata had never shared.

The list diverged from all the rest. The document was an official state record. Dated four years ago. Signed by Chancellor Charles, Founder of the State. The top page read:

EXTRAJUDICIAL EXECUTION

Daughter Frida Carlito - age fourteen
Daughter Juliette Marquez - age thirteen
Daughter Juliet Saramago - age twelve
Cristina Carlito - age forty-one
Elizabeth Marquez - age forty
Gabriella Saramago - age forty-two

Uncle Stigmata had been a busy boy. He had compiled detailed surveillance records on all six. What they ate for breakfast. How many times they went to the grocery store. What time they left the house every day. Who they associated with. Class schedules. Phone numbers and addresses of close friends and relatives. They even tracked their menstrual cycles through a digital app and knew their entire browser histories. For instance, Uncle Stigmata had made a note about Juliet

Saramago visiting a cute and cuddly site for baba foots a hundred times in thirty-eight hours. Most of her browsing history was cute and cuddly animals. They kept records of everyone.

"These people are sick," Leonor mumbled to herself.

The state knew every detail of their lives. *Why didn't the state assassinate us already?* The document labeled Cristina Carlito as "Commander 1." Then Gabriella Saramago as "Commander 2," and so on.

Leonor did the unthinkable and called Cristina Carlito. Even though the Mothers controlled Mafia Land now. The Land of Kings had fallen. Uncle Stigmata could still somehow manage deep state business from afar.

In a matter of hours, the Mothers arrived at Uncle Stigmata's home. They didn't arrive alone. They brought company. People trained in extracting important information from state sympathizers. Assassins like Leonor. If the Land of Kings still had sympathizers roaming the land, the Mothers would find them.

The Mothers didn't know how to approach the situation. They knew Mika, Leonor's mother, but not Uncle Stigmata. Uncle Stigmata had escaped capture because he was part of the deep state. The state kept poor records of deep state officials.

Uncle Stigmata's home was elegant and massive. Filled with many rooms and lavatories. Most rooms were empty. Besides cobwebs and dust orbs. Which glided across the floor when the furnace kicked on at noon.

The west wing of the house had a different vibe. Kettlebells, weightlifting machinery, punching bags, swords, batons, tasers, and animal prods filled every corner. Designed for combat training.

Once a week, Uncle Stigmata electrocuted Leonor with an animal prod. For insurance. He claimed. If the moment should arise, she would be ready to defend herself against tasers and prods. "A target will use just about anything to escape their fate," Uncle Stigmata repeatedly said before tasering her.

Seating at Uncle Stigmata's house was sparse. The dining room was the only stocked room in the house. The Mothers, after being invited inside, sat at a long rectangular table.

Mother Saramago sat at the edge of her seat. Her posture was straight. She was careful not to lean back too far. She placed her hands in her lap, as though she didn't know what else to do with them. Mother Carlito sat at the head of the table. While Leonor sat on the opposite end.

"We knew your mother well, Leonor." Mother Carlito raised her hands, gesturing to the other Mothers. "Mika was a visionary. Mafia Land wouldn't be possible without her."

Leonor's eyes rose when she heard her mother's name. She hadn't heard it in some time. Uncle Stigmata never mentioned her or father. Except during the memorial service. After that, he acted as though they never existed. He behaved as though he were Leonor's paternal father.

Mother Saramago chimed in by raising a hand. "Leonor, we didn't know Stigmata was a part of the deep state." She strained her eyes, looking perplexed. "We thought you and Addy would be safer in Stigmata's care."

"We made a promise to keep you and Addy safe."

"Addy's gone," Leonor scowled. "Uncle Stigmata…he trained me as an assassin."

"An assassin?" Mother Marquez's voice perked.

"I'm a girl." Leonor was on the verge of tears. "No one would ever suspect me." Her tone mocked Uncle Stigmata. *How could uncle betray me*, she kept thinking.

Mother Marquez was hesitant to meet Leonor at first. She spilled all her assassin exploits readily. Mother Marquez suspected a setup. Though now, watching Leonor come to tears relieved her apprehension. *She must feel guilty for all the killing*, Mother Marquez decided. *And if she feels guilty, then the girl has a heart*. Yet Mother Marquez harbored no guilt for her transgressions. She slept well at night. Snoring half the time. She, for a lack of a better word, was proud of her doings.

Little did Mother Marquez know, her transgressions did not cause Leonor's tears. She never felt guilty after taking a life. No, Leonor's watery eyes resulted from not knowing what would become of Uncle Stigmata.

Uncle Stigmata had delivered the news of her parents. They held a memorial service. Then the funeral. Then the burial. Then two days later, Uncle Stigmata told the girls to pack light while they were playing with their food at lunchtime. Addy and Leonor were too sad to eat a thing. They just sat there staring at their plates. Shuffling food with their forks. Sometimes piling everything to the left. Then sliding everything to the right. The entire house was dead. The only sound heard was their flatware occasionally scraping the plate.

Everything had happened so fast. Leonor had no time to think. To grieve. Uncle Stigmata had expected them to just move on as though everything were normal. Addy only cried when they turned in for the night. When the lights went out. And the house settled. She cried so quietly that Leonor could barely hear the sniffles.

She did her best not to disturb Leonor. Or break her. Addy covered her mouth as the tears flowed. Leonor knew Addy had covered her mouth because her nostrils whistled every time she breathed in.

Leonor had heard every tear fall from Addy's little face while feigning sleep. Her mind was wide awake, replaying the last day she had seen her parents alive. She didn't kiss them goodbye before leaving. Never said, "I love you," before slamming the front door behind.

She was late for class that cloudy day and needed to report to Mr. Alto at seven. Right before the bell rang. Not that they learned much. They forbade girls from being instructors. But Mr. Alto picked one lucky girl every month to be an instructor for the day. Mr. Alto had picked her for the first time in two years. Leonor was dead set on claiming her prize.

"Why come forward now, girl?" Mother Saramago rested her back against the chair. "You could have easily killed us if you wanted to. You still could." Mother Saramago nervously laughed.

"Mother Saramago is right." Mother Marquez's tone was raspy. She, too, adjusted. The Mothers appeared more relaxed than before.

"How can you go from plotting our death to handing over Stigmata on a golden platter?"

"He didn't tell me Addy died." Leonor held back tears. "He murdered them, you know."

The Mothers looked confused.

Mother Marquez squinted. "I thought kids texted each other every second. I can't get Juliette to put down the phone."

Leonor tossed her hand in the air. "Look at this place. Uncle Stigmata avoids technology at all cost. He feared surveillance would get him caught."

The Mothers averted their eyes and gave the house a once-over. Yes, Stigmata's home seemed to have been transported to a long-forgotten world. It also appeared the Mothers had forgotten how things once were in Land of Kings.

Mother Saramago was so laser focused on Leonor she hadn't noticed the state of the house. When Leonor dragged it into the light, Mother Saramago realized Leonor didn't behave like a typical teenager. She was a killer, no doubt. Though she had an undeniable innocence. She didn't act as though the Mothers had freed women.

Leonor's reaction to her sister's suicide may have seemed odd. But on closer inspection, Uncle Stigmata had betrayed Leonor from the start. A deeply painful betrayal. Now Leonor sought revenge.

Uncle Stigmata was methodical in everything he did. Unless it came to matters of the heart. A teenage heart at that. Leonor could communicate with Addy through letters. Allowing Uncle Stigmata to be the middleman. His preferred method. That was how he had gained control over the State Department. A plain old middleman wouldn't satisfy their needs.

As usual, Stigmata wanted more. Why he was the person Leonor had been writing to all along. Not Addy. Uncle Stigmata indulged these little fantasies of theirs. Wrote back as Leonor or Addy. Whenever the occasion called for it.

The girls weren't writing letters to each other, as they believed. Poured their hearts out too. Their most private thoughts, scribbled on paper twice a week, were read by Stigmata. The charade would have continued had it not been for Uncle Stigmata taking a sabbatical once Addy died. The poor schmuck got sloppy. "Do you know how exhausting it is for a man to pretend to be a teenage girl? Much less correspond with a pubescent child, week after week. Hour after hour?" He held two fingers in the air while spilling his guts to a bartender in one of those seedy joints. "Two pubescent girls. Two!"

Yes, Leonor had uncovered many things while snooping through Uncle Stigmata's study. Uncle Stigmata had trained Leonor as though she were the hired help. Not family. Every conversation they had revolved around training to kill. Concocting the perfect poison. Strict discipline, that bordered subservient. Eating healthy. Last, but not least, getting a good night's rest.

"Sound mind, sound body," he loved to scream while Leonor weaved through a maze of obstacles in under a minute.

He never once shared anything personal. Not once did he discuss growing up with their father. The hardship of becoming a man. He was professional to a fault. A businesslike attitude, as if he were building a killing machine he later introduced to the world. Leonor knew little of Uncle Stigmata's life before he became, well, Stigmata.

But she knew one thing for sure: Uncle Stigmata loathed the Mothers. He said, "I'll kill those treasonous bitches," whenever Leonor mentioned the Mothers.

The Mothers' rebellion that lead to defeat tortured his warped mind. He was obsessed. He plotted their deaths, day and night. Why, every day he came up with creative ways to kill the Mothers. One more gruesome than the next. Leonor had intended to balance things out. He had betrayed her first. She would surrender him to the enemy. That was that.

If Leonor delivered the final blow and sent him off to the great unknown, then the impact would be uneventful. He'd chalk the whole thing up as a gifted pupil becoming the master. Maybe even take the credit. Then, somewhere in his diseased brain, he could start living his best afterlife. Knowing Leonor had commissioned his death.

But, if Uncle Stigmata died at the hands of the Mothers. That betrayal would follow him straight to the underworld. *If there is an afterlife*, Leonor thought. Uncle Stigmata wouldn't die in peace if the Mothers took his life.

Mother Saramago laid a locket of hair on the table. The Mothers' eyes beamed as though someone had spilled a secret. "This will not right the wrong, Leonor. We should have investigated Stigmata." Mother Saramago slid the locket tied to zigzag silk. "Nothing will ever take the place of a mother. The dreams she aspires for her children."

"Gab," Mother Carlito said.

Mother Saramago held out her hand. "You're no longer Stigmata's pupil. No longer a Ferrante. You are a Saramago. My house is now your home. Because you spared our life." She glared at the Mothers. Mother Marquez wore a guilty face. "That locket entitles you to any oath you choose."

"Gab!" Mother Carlito slammed her fist on the table, causing the spider wood to vibrate and echo. Mother Carlito's graceful hands were deceiving and packed with power.

Mother Carlito's eyes glinted hard. Mother Marquez shrugged when she heard Mother Saramago relinquish oath. Her eyes sort of rolled. They didn't roll out of annoyance, rather rolled to say, "sounds about right."

"What will happen to Uncle? I mean, Stigmata."

"It's best you don't know," Mother Marquez said.

Mother Carlito stood. "I disagree. Like it or not," she turned to face Leonor, "Stigmata has destroyed this girl's life."

"Don't forget about Mom…Dad…Addy." The list would never end with Stigmata.

Mother Carlito's eyes went wide. Her expression was priceless. "I think, under the circumstance, Leonor should decide his fate."

The Mothers wore faces of agreement. Mother Marquez nodded, her lips scrunched. The Mothers fell in line, as they do. As they always did. They watched Leonor, awaiting her reply.

Leonor's face turned pink. All eyes were on her the pressure to decide Stigmata's fate was in her hands. It had been a long time since anyone asked her what she wanted.

Stigmata had dictated her entire existence. Destroyed her family. And yet, through loyalty, Stigmata was blood. She even grew to love the man and all his eccentricities. He was an enigma. And soon, she'd learn just how deep his enigma goes.

"I think he should pay."

Mother Marquez bounced to her feet with a smile.

"What about prison?" Leonor's voice was more confident this time, as though she had figured it out. "Can't you just lock him up?" She smacked her forehead as though she had gotten something wrong.

Mother Marquez frowned and sat. Mother Carlito looked disappointed while Mother Saramago eyed the Mothers. "There are no right answers. There never will be. He deserves death, considering the facts."

"It's foolish to keep him alive." Mother Marquez stood again. "He might escape. There are plenty of sympathizers out there willing to give their life for him."

Mother Carlito raised her hand. "The girl has decided. We'll interrogate him first." She gave the Mothers a look. "Stigmata will pay for his sins. Then we'll find a suitable prison. Seneca might house him for a few years until we—"

"House him," Mother Marquez said.

Mother Carlito gave Mother Marquez razor eyes. She then placed eyes on Leonor. "I understand he trained you in the assassin's ways."

"Yeah," Leonor said. She was foolish to follow him. Hand delivering all those death notes like a domesticated baba foot. Never second-guessing the master of the house. She showed signs of regret. Though below the surface, she regretted nothing. She had convinced herself the assassin's life was a good death.

"Then stay for the interrogation."

"Cris!" Mother Saramago stood.

"She's an assassin."

"I doubt she's seen this kind of interrogation before. Believe you me."

Mother Carlito rolled her eyes and peered at Leonor. "Would you like to stay?"

"Yeah," Leonor said. "I want to hear what he has to say."

Mother Saramago flailed her hands, shook her head, and sat with arms folded.

"Then it's settled. Are we in agreement?"

The Mothers inched a finger skyward. Though Mother Marquez gave Leonor a suspicious eye. She empathized with Leonor's request to spare Stigmata's life. At the same time, she wondered about Leonor's decision to stay. But somewhere deep down, she understood it.

It was a contradiction on Leonor's part, for sure. Mother Marquez didn't like contradictions. You either wanted him out of harm's way or wished him dead. You couldn't have it both ways. That contradiction alarmed Mother Marquez.

It was more than that. There was something creepy about Leonor's voice. Using that little, helpless voice to gain sympathy. She was a killer trapped inside a teenager's body. A natural-born death note dealer. And there's no remedy for that. There's only one remedy for bloodlust—more blood.

Mother Falls & Daughters Rise

THE INTIMATE KILL technique is best used for high-profile targets. Ninety-nine percent of the time, the victim dies from blood loss after the jugular is severed. Mother Carlito was the 1 percent who lived.

Like the potions, Leonor had perfected slicing a juggler. If one cuts too deep, the victim bleeds out in seconds. She didn't care for that method. She liked to savor the between stages. When life teases death. The eyes do something funny when the lights fade.

What Leonor discovered: agile hands, armed with a surgeon's touch, can slice the throat so the victim bleeds out slowly. It's psychological warfare for a target to fight for their life. Then make peace with their inevitable end. She loved the intimacy of a slow death. One complication arose. 1 percent of victims survived. She had no way of calculating the odds because death was unpredictable. Fate is, well, fate. And God's plans are mysterious. Mortals don't have godlike power. Everyone in Mafia Land knew that.

Mother Carlito lay in the hospital bed, unable to articulate. During the argument, Leonor had severed one of her vocal cords. Which doctors later stitched. Leonor had severed other important nerves. The way Mother Carlito had collapsed after Leonor had cut her throat had saved her life. Or, rather, the way Leonor had rudely pushed her the other way.

Her neck was at an odd angle when she sunk into the cushion. It stopped the bleeding but caused more damage. If not for that, Mother Carlito would be a corpse.

Leonor did not fare better. The ICU crash team had visited her three times in less than six hours. Enough time for one sun to crawl past the high county. She required heavy doses of transfusions because Mother Carlito had pierced her liver and nicked a kidney. To say she cut deep would be a gross understatement of the highest order.

If Mafia Land wasn't small enough. It seemed, in Leonor's predicament, shrunk to the size of a blunder beetle. The only person with her blood type triple O-positive to the fifth power pulsed inside Frida Carlito's veins. The land's bloodshed mandated blood type registration for all. And often called to duty in cases such as these.

Frida Carlito readily donated blood for Leonor. In mass quantities. She instructed the hospital staff to feed her a special diet to enrich the plasma with important nutrients. Frida's act of kindness wasn't altruistic. She had planned for one purpose: save Leonor, only to kill her in the arena. No double take required. Frida Carlito nursed Leonor back to health only to kill her.

Leonor had stolen too much from Frida. And, as the newly appointed Mother, Leonor's actions were unforgivable. Frida Carlito was pregnant too. Her secret love was dead. Plus Mother Carlito's life teetered toward the afterlife.

Frida sat beside Mother Carlito's infirmary bed, clinging to her hand. "I'm not ready to be Mother." Tears in her eyes. Her gaze averted down toward the floor.

Mother Carlito flailed her hand. "Look…at…me." Her voice was all jabberwocky. Her voice box seemed removed and replaced with an artificial larynx. She pointed. "You…are…ready." Mother Carlito rested her hand over her throat. Then etched a pained face.

"Don't talk." Frida stroked her Mother's forehead. "You'll pull through. You'll see."

Though Mother Carlito had seen something in Frida's eyes that told a different tale. She didn't believe Mother would recover. Mother Carlito shook her head. The pain in her neck was excruciating. "Not… this time."

"I'm not ready," Frida said. "I need you."

Frida lowered her head and cried. Mother Carlito smacked the steel bed rail. Making a clinking noise with her ring. Frida looked up. "You…are wiser than…" Mother Carlito couldn't finish the sentence. She pointed at herself to complete the statement. She shook her head again. "Do…it…your…way."

"Eye for an Eye."

Mother Carlito's face melted with fear. "Leo…nor…ass…assin." She gripped her throat and swallowed. "Won't…win."

The fear brewing in Mother Carlito's eyes compelled Frida to flinch. But she refused to heed the warning. "I don't care."

"Mia," Mother Carlito garbled.

Before Frida could reply, Mother Saramago and Mother Marquez rushed into the room. "Cris," Mother Saramago said. "How could you? You granted Leonor oath. *Oath.*"

Mother Carlito beamed dagger eyes. "I…had…no…choice."

"Choice." Mother Marquez snickered. "Now what, war?"

Frida stood. "Fight for life."

Frida's careless statement silenced the Mothers. Mother Carlito slapped her forehead and rolled her eyes.

"You won't survive in the arena." Mother Saramago glared at Frida. "Leonor is Stigmata's protégé."

"Stigmata?" Frida glanced at Mother Carlito. In return, a guilty expression hung on Mother Carlito's face. "Who's Stigmata, Mother?"

"Don't worry about him." Mother Marquez's voice radiated from behind. Her crusty voice rose over their shoulders. "Leonor is a gifted death dealer."

Frida turned to face the Mothers when Mother Carlito couldn't answer the question. "Who's Stigmata?"

While Frida's back was turned, Mother Carlito shook her head and silenced the Mothers.

"You mustn't concern yourself with Stigmata." Mother Saramago paced. "Just know Leonor is deadly. She's skilled at delivering a death note like nothing I've seen before. You're not a trained killer. You must call it off immediately."

"I'm pregnant!"

The Mothers gasped.

"Here we go again," Mother Marquez said while mimicking a rolling-eye emoji.

Mother Saramago massaged her temple.

Mother Carlito smacked the rail again, urging all to look. "I... forbid—"

"I'm Mother now." Frida's pride had foolishly inflated beyond recognition. "I will end Leonor for good."

Sometimes the devil you know isn't the devil you know well. By *well*, I mean, not at all. Sometimes the devil you know is deadlier than the original estimate. Miscalculations troubled by pride and arrogance.

And before the Mothers could say another word, a nurse burst through the door, panting. A look of shock came upon her. "Leonor Saramago," the nurse sucked in more air, "is," almost there, "going to make it."

"Shit." Mother Marquez snapped her fingers.

"Rise." Mother Saramago motioned to Frida. "You shall rise, daughter. You will soon discover the true weight of Mother."

* * *

Remedios was an ordinary child. From ordinary parents. Garden-variety childhood home. Safe, common neighborhood. Best put, her world was nothing extraordinary. Inside and out.

But she had a special gift. She could detect bullshit, supernaturally. Not only could she sniff out a lie, but some said she could read the soul like a book. The secrets people keep locked inside the heart. A heart that welcomes anything to live inside.

Remedios took a liking to Leonor at first. She, too, thirsted for blood. She had a love named Magenta. Magenta had died in the long war. Not during battle. She was sound asleep when the dirty bomb blew up her childhood home. Leonor looked much like Magenta. Even their mannerisms matchbooked.

Yet, Leonor, on the inside, was nothing like Magenta. "Leonor," as Remedios had put it, "is like a three-headed blue thumper with the heart of Lamash."

The more Remedios hung out with Leonor, the more she realized just how evil to the bone she was. She had dark goals for real. Like for real, real. She had no rizz. Not like Juliet Saramago. Who Leonor loathed to pieces. She was still part of the squad. A made girl.

Before they strung Devin to the wall, Remedios had trailed Leonor secretly, tracking Leonor's whereabouts. Strange enough, Leonor always ended up at Seneca Institute. Who the hell was she visiting there?

Although, before visiting the institute, Leonor would meet Tetchy at a trashy motel on the outskirts. Remedios spied Tetchy and Leonor's escapades through the room's sheer curtains. It wasn't hard to see every detail unfold beyond those paper-thin sheers. Was it love? Or just chillin'? Remedios didn't want to know the answer. Determining Leonor's state of love proved difficult. Or if she was playing some sick game. She lived a double life outside Mafia Land.

Whatever her motivation. It had to be more devious than just chillin' with a made dude. Tetchy and Leonor met up almost every night. At the same motel. Room 888.

It had to be more than just sex. Even though they smashed like fairy turtles. Going at it for half the night. The rest of the time, Tetchy lay in Leonor's arm. Remedios could hear them whispering about all kinds of stuff. Stuff they dare not speak about.

Tetchy would sob. Two days before Tetchy's murder, Remedios had heard him say he'd leave Frida Carlito for good. On that same night, Remedios followed Leonor inside the institute. Where she first heard the name Stigmata. The lobby was a futuristic spectacle. Clean lines and blinding white. Machines automated everything. A starship came to mind.

She hid outside the institute. Inside a cluster of shrubs. And waited for Leonor to leave the building. Once Leonor left, Remedios went back inside. She told the red-faced guard that sat behind the energy shield window, "I'm here to see Stigmata."

The red-faced guard inspected Remedios. He punched a few words into the computer. "Stand perfectly still. Face recognition will tell me everything I need to know."

"Even face recognition can be hacked" Remedios seemed confused. She yanked the emblem from her shirt. "You see this? This is the House of Saramago."

"You must be on the list."

"I'm Leonor Saramago."

The red-faced guard cracked a smile. His eyes droopy, unenthused. "Try again."

"Mother Saramago."

The red-faced guard scratched his bald head, annoyed. "Stand still please."

Remedios glared at the lens. A blue laser scanned her face. Within seconds, a delicious chime sounded.

He wore disappointment, as though someone had spat in his face. "You're approved."

Remedios appeared as shocked as the red-faced guard. "Of course I am."

"Visiting hours are from three to ten." He glanced at the holographic screen. "It's 10:03."

"I'm not leaving until I talk to Stigmata."

A pencil-framed guard materialized from nowhere and said, "Is there a problem here?"

* * *

At three sharp the next day, Remedios visited Stigmata. The institution bore the likeness of the arena prison. Strangely, a high-tech wellness club for the rich came to mind. The prisoners wore exotic leisure suits. Some leaned toward spacesuits.

Most prisoners came and went. Guards patrolled every station. Although most leaned against walls. Bored out of their minds. Some played on their phones without looking up.

Every guard was weaponless. Strange to see nothing dangerous strapped to their waists. What if an incursion broke out? The guards were a mere afterthought. Decorations sprinkled around for optics.

Remedios knew better. Seneca's technology outranked Mafia Land. Any land on the planet. In every field. Their algorithms were so advance, it could zap a prisoner for farting in the sterilized zone. Not by a guards hand. But by a sadistic AI network.

A guard chaperoned Remedios to parking space seven-zero-seven. A little too close for comfort. She could feel his breath tickling the back of her neck. *Parking space*, Remedios thought. *What's Seneca coming to next?* The seventh floor had a different vibe than the ground level.

She got the creeps from each parking space she passed. Invisible boxes with blue outlines etched on the floor. Guards confined prisoners inside them. Stretching as far as the eye could see. Unlike ground level, these prisoners weren't free to roam. These futuristic contraptions suspended each prisoner. Like a bug frozen inside an ice cube.

Inside the blue, square outline, parking space seven-zero-seven, a man sat at a desk. Back facing Remedios. The invisible box was minimal. A desk with a chair. No toilet. Remedios wondered, *How do they go to the bathroom?*

A guard sat in a chair in front of parking space seven-zero-seven. She placed her hand out. "Visitors must steer clear from the energy shield. It will paralyze. Remain seated during visitation. Don't stand unless instructed. Standing is an act of aggression."

Stigmata slid the chair out from the desk and stood. "If I were you, I'd listen. You might find yourself locked inside an invisible box if you don't, my child."

Remedios sat, afraid to get too close. She studied Stigmata. "Why does Leonor Saramago visit you every day?"

"Leonor was Ferrante way before Saramago."

"Don't play games, old man."

"The hard way it is, my child." Stigmata sat back down and scribbled something on paper. Back facing Remedios.

Remedios glared and thought about what to say next. "Why am I on the visitor's list?"

"Now we're getting somewhere." Stigmata turned to face Remedios. "You've been watching her. But you've stumbled into a spider's reach, I'm afraid."

"What does that mean?"

Stigmata went nose to outline. His breath fogged the spot-free energy shield. His eyes sparkled through the fog. Remedios could see deep scars layered on his face. His left eye was partly cloudy. "Not too bright, I see."

Remedios scooted the chair close. The metal legs screeched across the concrete floor. "Quit playing games, and tell me the truth, old man."

"You've been watching her, but in reality, she's been watching you. She tells me you'd make a fine addition." He smiled big. Pleased with himself.

"You will not alter my brain chemistry, old man."

"Is she right?" Stigmata's eyes glinted past the foggy energy shield like a star breaking through the Milky Way. "Are you ready to join?"

Remedios sat there like a three-headed blue thumper. Thinking and biting her nails. "No."

Stigmata raised a brow. "Neutrality is safe. But, eventually, one must choose a side. People make rash decisions in stressful situations. It's best to choose now. While your mind is fresh. Rather than make a poor decision later. Who knows, you might not get another chance to strike." He fluttered his fingers as if a strand of hair was tangled in his hand.

"I'm done here."

The guard folded the chair. When Remedios was ready to leave, Stigmata said, "Is Mafia Land truly better than the Land of Kings? Sometimes the lines are so blurry you can't tell the new from the old. Something to think about on your way home."

No, Remedios thought, *Stigmata is mistaken*, as she rode the elevator down. *Mafia Land is nothing like the Land of Kings*. Though, something inside Remedios said he might be right. She rushed out of the lobby and onto the street. And who did she bump into? Leonor. She was sitting on a retaining wall near the sidewalk, as though she were expecting Remedios to emerge from the institution.

Remedios masked her surprise as best she could. "Stigmata is totally shady." She motioned a hand to emphasize. "Who is he?"

"I thought he would tell you?"

Remedios didn't answer. Instead, she glared at Leonor.

"He's my uncle."

"You just can't keep the lies straight."

"Who do you think put him here?"

"Were we ever friends?" Remedios pounded her fist into her palm. "Or was that a lie, too?"

Leonor's eyes wandered past Remedios's shoulder as if something else had grabbed her attention. "He tried to eliminate the Mothers."

"That's totally shady. Sneaking around and shit."

"The Mothers know." Leonor paused. Trying to read Remedios's mind. "You don't believe me?"

Remedios kept staring dead-eyed at Leonor.

"Ask them yourself."

"So this is how it goes?" Remedios said. "Are you squad? Or are you with him?"

Leonor cracked a smile. "We'll see."

"Leonor!"

"The question is, Remedios, are *you* squad?" Leonor gave her a funny expression. "I mean, lately it seems like you're not happy with the way things are turning out. The Mothers can be a little much, don't you think?" Leonor placed a hand high and the other low. "You were squad, way up here. But now they turned you into a death dealer, way down here. So are you squad or a death dealer? You can't be both, can you?"

"You got me fucked up. I'm made."

"Are you, though?" Leonor got in Remedios's face. "Last time I checked, made girls don't death deal." Remedios smelled a hint of pepper nips on Leonor's breath.

"Made girls have to death deal sometimes. It's oath."

"I don't death deal. Juliet Marquez doesn't death deal. Come to think of it," Leonor pointed at Remedios's chest, "you're the only one in the squad who death deals."

"I death deal because I'm good at it."

"The Mothers may see you as a death dealer," Leonor tucked her long bangs behind her ear, "but I see you as a CEO girl. Not a fucking death dealer." Leonor pretended to balance something in her hands. "Are you a fucking meal, or are you a CEO? Just saying."

"Who the fuck are you?" Remedios said, tears in her eyes. "Are you a fucking CEO of Mafia Land? Are you the CEO of anything? You're not pushing anything. Running around like you do. Acting shady."

"Like it or not," Leonor toggled her finger between them, "you and I are outsiders, period."

Travelogue

The *three-headed blue thumper* is a symbol of peace. Warm and silky creatures with diamond eyes that are cuddly and cute and rare. People only see a handful each year. Beheadings to anyone caught poaching these creatures for their diamond eyes.

The *Lamash* is a demon. Not to be confused with *Lamashtu*—Mesopotamia. Which looks like a demon and wreaks havoc on the land. And causes women to miscarry. And drinks the blood of men and eats their flesh. Mafia Land *Lamash* seems childlike. Approachable. But if one gets close, it will consume the soul and leave a human shell in its wake.

The *fairy turtles* are the color of snow. But unlike the three-headed blue thumper, fairy turtles mate every six hours. Their circadian rhythm relies on four suns. And they spend most of their lives mating in most frightful ways, as though competing in fight for life. They zip around so fast, traveling from one partner to the next, that it sours the stomach of anyone who dares peek. They have no pants to zip up in a hurry. Which raises the question: if they did, would they? They produce many offspring that overcrowd the seaside and are a trouble-some bunch. Some call them "hooligans by the sea." Though they are garbage disposals of the sea and filtrate waterways. Mafia Land wouldn't have access to clean water without those troublemakers.

Tories the Rebirth

"WE'RE prepared to make adjustments for the state," Charles said. "If we're to build something greater, Stigmata and I realize women play a vital role in our society." He handed Leonor a hologram-stick.

Remedios and Leonor gave each other a strange look.

"Uncle Stigmata thinks chancellors are obsolete," Leonor said.

He furrowed in contemplation. "I don't believe Stigmata and I have ever discussed such matters." Charles swiveled his chair, turning his back on the girls. "I suppose he's right. We should elevate chancellor status to dictator. I like the sound of that."

After the long war, Charles had fled to the countryside on the outskirts of Seneca. Rio de la Plata, to be precise. He escaped capture with the help of Salvador. Who managed Charles's wealth and changed his identity.

Charles's villa was modest compared to his lavish crib in Land of Kings. "Nine hundred and twelve square feet. Two bedrooms. One bath. It's not suitable for a man of my stature," he had muttered one day while sipping fig bubbles and wearing that blunder beetle robe. The one infested by fairy lice and eaten to threads.

He had turned one bedroom into an office. Where Remedios and Leonor sat now. But he had to make do. Now that his wealth had tanked in the war. His riches shrank to twenty native irons for every brick because of the war. Charles had lost a lot of bricks. Plus Salvador's usual fees for service. The devil always collects dues. Even if one pays in their own blood.

Still, he hired a house attendant from a nearby village. He had done nothing for himself in decades. An army of attendants did everything for him. That was something he wouldn't compromise.

If he did all his own chores, he might as well move back into his childhood home. If it still existed. They scraped it off like the other structures to make room for those up-and-coming communities. Somewhere in his mind, he thought, *my childhood home was better than this blabber hoof shack.*

"I think Uncle Stigmata is done with all that." Leonor looked at Remedios and winked. "He's preparing for the future."

"Done with all that?" Charles mocked. "Preparing for the future? What kind of future will there be without a dictator?" He turned to face the girls and tapped his finger on the desk. "This land requires an iron fist." He lifted his hands. "Otherwise, you're paddling the same boat."

Charles said, *this land,* as though he were still living in the Land of Kings. As though he had forgotten where he lived. The house attendant interrupted the meeting by asking, "Can I get you another cup of tar beans, Chancellor?"

Charles sprung and raised an angry hand. The attendant winced and hunkered. "Away with you, boy. You dare interrupt me while I speak."

Leonor examined the boy. Who wasn't a boy. Maybe a boy compared to Charles. She found the house attendant attractive as she stared him down with lustful eyes. Very attractive.

"Yes, Chancellor. I apologize," he said, scuttling out of the room.

"Where was I before that imbecile interrupted?"

Leonor rose. Looked at Remedios and winked again. "You're such a boomer, Charles. You're not the future. That boy's got more future in his pinkie."

"Boomer." Charles's superior tone echoed. "I never understood your generation's tongue. It's all so...so...," he placed a finger on his lips, "Nonsensical."

"It means you're spoiled," Leonor chimed in.

"Yeah." Remedios smiled. "Out of date. La...la...la...la..."

"Has she lost her mind?" Chancellor glared at Leonor.

"She does that."

"Well, tell her to stop at once."

"La...la...la...la..."

Leonor palmed Remedios to stop. "She says it's time to punch your clock."

Charles's angry face melted into a somber expression. "You can't hand me a death note. This is neutral ground. Why, you couldn't even."

A loud bang echoed. Ringing everyone's ears in the room. The smell of gunpowder filled the space. Charles screamed in agony as the bullet plowed dead center of his chest. Shattering bone. He clutched his white shirt while blood pooled.

The house attendant heard the gunshot from the kitchen while scrubbing dishes. Even heard Charles scream. But ignored the cry for help.

"La...la...la...la." Remedios was still aiming the gun at Charles.

"You little bitch, you shot me," Charles said, high-pitched, as though he couldn't believe what Remedios had done. The betrayal was so overwhelming that his eyes went wild. He screamed again, still clutching his chest. Blood oozing through his fingers like a cheap elixir. He looked like a man on the verge of death. Correction, he looked like a man who knew he was going to die at any second.

Leonor removed the gun from Remedios's hand. "You're not a death dealer no more."

"La...la ..." Remedios crinkled her nose and peered at Leonor. "What do you call this?"

"You're dealing for yourself now."

"So, basically I'm a death dealer for Stigmata," Remedios glared at Leonor.

"Stigmata," Charles said between the throes of death. "We had an agreement." Still gripping his white shirt, he glared for a second longer. Shock riddling his face. Then he laid his head on the desk.

"What about the boy?" Remedios nodded toward the kitchen.

Leonor gave her that look. A look that required no words. "I don't do that kind of shit. I never kill innocents."

"Fine." Leonor walked toward the door and winked. "You do you. I'll do me."

Remedios grabbed Leonor's arm. She peeled her hand open. "I'll do it."

Leonor smiled and slapped the gun in Remedios's hand. "Make it quick. We don't want to be late."

Remedios waited for Leonor to exit the front door. She locked eyes on the boy. He was still scrubbing a mountain of dishes. Humming away, listening to music. "Haven't you heard of the laser washer?"

The boy flinched midscrub. Then turned to meet Remedios's gaze. "Chancellor Charles says cleanliness is next to godliness."

"You listen to that boomer?"

"Handwashing is better."

Remedios rolled her eyes. "That's bullshit. Everybody knows lasers sterilize dishes better than soap and water." she gave a look. "It doesn't waste a drop of water. That cheap ass."

"Mom says the same thing."

"Okay, then." Remedios grew annoyed, revealing her palm. "Stop doing the fucking dishes and listen up." The gun sensor built a ferocious chime.

Fear infected the boy's face. Remedios pointed the gun at the floor. "Get down on your hands and knees. When I nod, you scream. Like your life depends on it. Got it?"

"Why?" The boy's voice was shaky.

She pointed the gun at the front door. "You see that girl?"

He bobbed his head.

"She wants me to kill you."

Tears welled.

"I won't do that. I just want her to think I did. Got it?"

He nodded again, this time faster than before.

"I'm pressed for time, understand?"

The boy stared at Remedios with pitiful eyes and squinted. Remedios nodded, the boy screamed, and the gun rocked the house.

* * *

Remedios shut the door behind.

"Took you long enough."

Remedios walked past Leonor and sat in the passenger seat of an air transit. Leonor deployed the wings and readied for takeoff.

"Don't get pissy." Leonor looked at Remedios. "Never leave a witness alive."

"Next stop, Mother Saramago," she screamed over the whirring engines.

Leonor scrutinized Remedios. "No, Uncle Stigmata."

Remedios peeked at her phone. "Visiting hours are almost over. We won't make it."

"We need to tell him the good news."

Remedios crossed her legs and folded her arms. "Mother Saramago wants me to report back." Mother Saramago did not request to see Remedios.

Leonor removed a hologram-stick from her pocket and handed it to Remedios. "Uncle Stigmata despised Charles. He only befriended him to get the list of Tories. This stick has the entire network." The aerial transit ascended with a hum. "What you hold in your hand will destroy a nation."

"What?"

"No one's safe."

* * *

The attendant announced Remedios's arrival to Mother Saramago.

"Yes, I'll allow it." Mother Saramago massaged platinum oil on her cheeks. "I'll meet her in the greenhouse."

"Yes, Mother."

Mother Saramago raised her hand. "Have Jinx join us. I imagine whatever Remedios has to say will intrigue him."

"Yes, Mother."

Mother Saramago gazed into the ancient vanity mirror. She patted the bags under her eyes with her fingertips. "You're getting old," she said to herself. "It's Juliet's time now."

"Would you like fig bubbles while you wait?"

Remedios shook her head.

The attendant wore love eyes and kept staring at Remedios. "How about a cup of tar beans? I can brew it fresh. It's no trouble."

"I'm good."

Before the attendant left the room, she said, "We're rooting for you." She lowered her eyes, blushing. "You're going to crush Mountain High."

Remedios swirled her eyes. "Yeah, thanks."

Mother Saramago didn't show up right away. She made Remedios wait in the greenhouse for some time. Jinx arrived before Mother Saramago.

Remedios sprung to her feet. "Where's Mother?"

Jinx gulped hard. "You know Mother."

Remedios plopped down on the velvety sofa, causing the cushions to sound with a loud puff. "What are you doing here?"

Jinx raised his hand to the light. Inspecting his fingernails. Blowing on his delicate fingertips as if he had gotten a manicure. "With Mother, you never know."

"I want to speak with Mother low-key."

He lounged on the adjacent sofa and rested his feet on the elixir table. "Mother keeps no secrets from me. You're acting a little sus. I hope all is well in the world. In *your* world."

Remedios landed hateful eyes on Jinx. "I'm loyal to Mother. Don't throw shade."

"Then why did Mother request my presence?" Jinx was still experimenting with his fingernails. "I never thought I'd see you fall from grace."

Remedios ascended and raised her fists to her hips. Jinx started laughing. His reaction baffled Remedios. She never lowered her hands.

"You should see the look on your face." He laughed, barely able to contain himself.

"One day, Jinx." Remedios brandished her fist. "You're going to fuck with the wrong girl. She's going to punch your clock. Then I'm goanna laugh."

"What's this about?" Mother Saramago raised her voice. Unbeknownst to Jinx and Remedios, their bickering was loud enough to flow outside the greenhouse. "We don't fight among each other. Remember this—we're family. I expect both of you to conduct yourselves as such."

Jinx sat at attention with a perfect posture. Remedios straightened too. "Yes, Mother," they said in perky unison.

"I asked Jinx to join us because I imagine whatever you've discovered about our Leonor he may need to investigate."

"Investigate," Jinx sarcastically muttered.

Mother Saramago looked at Jinx as if she would rip his head off. And everybody knew to never displease Mother. Her reaction turned his sneer into a frown.

Mother Saramago's fragrance dominated the room. Even though the greenhouse teamed with floral and plant scents. Mother used so many elixirs in her daily ritual she became a walking elixir. Juniper and the metallic scent of platinum, aligned with amber. All these elixirs leaked from her skin like gasoline vapors from the old world.

"Have you intercepted the Tories from the old land?" Mother Saramago motioned to the attendant standing nearby. "Brew some tar beans." She raised two fingers. Ajar and parallel, as if she were measuring centimeters. "This much blabber hoof milk." She peered at Jinx for a second, then at Remedios. "Brew enough for everyone."

Jinx made a face. "None for me."

Mother Saramago gave him that look. Causing him to shut his mouth.

"Now," Mother Saramago sat facing the two, "I hope you bring good news."

Remedios fished the hologram-stick from her pocket and held it to the light. "Leonor gave me this after I punched Chancellor Charles's clock."

Mother Saramago's eyes glistened. Excitement wearing her entire demeanor. She couldn't hide her glorious smile. "Really," she said. "He's finally dead?"

Jinx peered at Remedios in disbelief. "You... I don't believe it."

Mother sprang and paced, hand caressing her chin. "Are you sure it was Chancellor Charles? You confirmed his identity?"

"Yes." Remedios used a tone of pride. Rubbing Jinx's nose in her success. "Leonor gave this to me after I punched his clock. The entire network of Tories."

"Well." Mother Saramago sat and gestured at Remedios to lay the hologram-stick on the elixir table. "Let's see who's on the list, shall we?"

The moment Remedios laid the hologram-stick on the elixir table, a blue hologram emerged. Many files appeared. Thousands of names and addresses. Businesses in Seneca. Mountain, Valley, and River regions. "My, my." Mother thumbed through the files. "Stigmata has used his time wisely while incarcerated."

Jinx recognized a familiar name, Adlin Saramago, Juliet's cousin. His girlfriend of three years. Mother Saramago pored over the list. Not only did he pin Adlin Saramago. So did everybody else in the room. She wasn't the only sus on the list. Mother Marquez's name also appeared. Along with many others. Some were allies.

Jinx edged closer to the blue hologram. "How do we know this isn't a hoax? For all we know, Leonor could play us all. I mean, she suddenly confesses all her sins to Remedios." He angrily flicked his hand toward Remedios.

"Jinx," Mother Saramago ignored his tantrum, "assemble your best squad." She peered at Remedios. "If the list is accurate, Tories have infiltrated Mafia Land at the highest level."

Jinx shook his head. "This whole thing is sus." He pointed a damning finger at Remedios. "Why would Leonor trust you? You're sneaking around with Tories behind our back. How do we know you're not playing both sides?" He threw his hands in the air. "With… whatever this is."

"That's enough." Mother Saramago locked eyes on him. "Remedios has been playing double agent from the beginning. The moment Remedios caught Leonor visiting Stigmata."

"I'll deliver a death note Stigmata will never forget."

"No." Mother Saramago reached out her hand. "He's our only link to these Tories. We need to flush them out like the goblin smack they are. If he dies, they might go underground. Then we'll never rid the land of these Tories."

Jinx was about to say something when Juliet clicked through the greenhouse in long boots. She was wearing a masquerade costume. And an elaborate blunder beetle mask. Lilac feathers and sequins ruffled and created a symphony as she strutted.

"Juliet." Mother Saramago's brows furrowed. "Where are you going at this hour?"

"A rager." Juliet removed the mask, annoyed.

Mother Saramago stared at Juliet with a blank expression.

"The Baroness Mansion, remember?"

Two days before, Juliet had asked Mother's permission to go to the rager of a lifetime. A pre-celebration for clinching the finals—if they won one more match. Mother Saramago's expression appeared as though she didn't recall the conversation. Distracted by other matters at hand. "Oh, yes. Do be careful."

Mother didn't know that Juliet would go to the Baroness rager only to secretly meet someone she dare not associate with. And to further complicate matters, Juliet would fall in love with this secret someone.

Juliet stopped midstride and gave Remedios a strange look. "Aren't you coming?"

Remedios glanced at Mother Saramago, whose eyes swirled. "Uh, maybe later."

"Everyone's expecting you."

"I will." Remedios looked at Jinx. "I just have some things to do beforehand."

Juliet paused, inspecting everyone in the room. They were all wearing serious faces. "Did someone die or something?"

Mother Saramago stood. "Everything is fine." She shoed Juliet. "Enjoy the rager. Remedios will join you later."

Juliet was reluctant to leave and unsatisfied with Mother's response. Something was amiss. But she didn't know what. Still, she obeyed Mother's words. "See you there."

Juliet • Juliette = Love Rage

MUSIC SPILLED from the Baroness Mansion like a tidal wave. Lasers and interactive holograms transformed stone and mortar into a light show. Guests enjoyed copious amounts of fig bubbles, elixirs, and triple distilled drinks. Imported from Seneca. Tundra caviar and goblin smack heart. The skin of a glass-newt. The party eclipsed all others of the century.

Juliet had been eyeing the plague doctor from across the room. Nobody knew who was wearing the period costume. That couture outfit reigned supreme that evening. The boiled leather ankle coat was grimmer than an undertaker.

A brimmed hat made it difficult to see the person behind the deadly facade. Seductive eyes peered out from the beak mask. Those seductive eyes had eyeballed Juliet all night. Unknown to Juliet, the plague doctor was admiring her masquerade ensemble, too.

When the plague doctor bolted from the ballroom and headed toward the entryway, Juliet chased after. "Wait." Juliet grabbed the plague doctor's arm. "Don't go."

Hesitating, the plague doctor turned around.

"Where did you get that costume?"

The plague doctor locked eyes on Juliet, shook their head, and lifted their hands, as if to say, "who knows?"

"Come on." Juliet nudged the plague doctor on the shoulder. "It's the best one here."

The plague doctor didn't answer and tried to leave. Juliet saw something in those seductive eyes. Despite her uncertainty, it fascinated her. "Take off your mask."

"I can't," a female voice said, still peering at Juliet with those alluring eyes.

Juliet did something she never does. She twirled her hair. She had never played with her hair around Sebastian Carlito. Or Emilio Vicario, her eighth-grade crush.

The girl behind the mask smelled of juniper and platinum. The plague doctor tried to leave in a hurry again, but Juliet grabbed her hand. "Don't go. I've been waiting for you," Juliet said, wearing playful eyes you can't say no to.

The plague doctor grabbed Juliet and pulled her into a corridor near the spiral staircase. The plague doctor posed Juliet. Putting some distance between them. Juliet folded her arms and tilted her head as though trying to read the plague doctor's mind.

They gazed at each other. Then the plague doctor looked to the left, then right. Making sure the hallway was clear. "Promise not to laugh." The plague doctor removed that brimmed hat.

Juliet smiled. "I'd never do that. Unless you want me to." Her voice was smooth as silk.

The plague doctor removed the mask from her face. The timid girl behind the mask glued eyes to the floor and said, "Not what you were expecting?" She fixed her hair, thinking she didn't look presentable.

Juliet lifted the girl's chin to make eye contact. "I'm thinking I must be the luckiest girl here because of you."

"Seriously?" The girl smoothed her hair more, as though all the fidgeting in the world would fix her confidence.

Juliet stared at the girl with those inquisitive eyes. She could feel her blood channeling through the molecular machine at light speed.

Her cheeks burned. An odd tingle percolated inside her stomach. "Beautiful… You're beautiful."

A peculiar energy permeated the air. A gravitational pull that seemed to draw the two closer, like static electricity. A sharp spark that stings the brain. Then infects everything else. Juliette cradled the girl's cheek. In return, the girl placed a hand on top. Her shy brain went blank. The only thing she could think to say was, "Thank you."

"What's your name?"

"Seriously." Her eyes shied away. "You know my name."

"Juliette," Juliet whispered as though she couldn't believe they both had the same name.

"Yeah," Juliette Marquez said, furrowing her brow. "I love when you do that."

Juliet smiled. "Juliette," she said, louder this time, as though the whole thing was strangely comical. As though Mafia Land was a funny little place.

The two were just standing there. Consuming each other with those unsure, seductive eyes. Locked inside by some love spell. Nervous about going further. In reality, ready to tear those clothes off. "You never answered my question?"

Juliette Marquez stepped closer, touching chest to chest, and pulled a sequin from Juliet's hair. Juliette Marquez held it to the light. "This was stuck in your hair."

Juliet waited no longer and took full advantage of their proximity. In her mind, she believed Juliette Marquez had made the first move. Juliet devoured Juliette Marquez with a kiss. Like those lips fed her air. A kiss driven by impulse. Pheromones toxifying the air. Juliette Marquez's eyes went wide. She stared at Juliet, speechless.

Something about the way Juliette Marquez reacted to the kiss led Juliet to think she'd done something wrong. Juliet's eyes watered. "I'm sorry, I don't—"

Juliette Marquez kissed her back. This time longer and more passionately. The music faded into the background. All the laughter and voices and the people going by seemed to vanish. Mafia Land, so it seemed, only had enough room for the two. The scent of juniper. She tasted platinum layered somewhere between.

Reality and fate demanded a seat at the table. And would soon hurl Juliet and Juliette back to planet Mafia Land in two-point-two seconds. Just enough time for Tetchy to walk past them, making out in the corridor, on his way to the bathroom, or so he claimed. "Fig bubbles runs right through me," he had screamed at Devin minutes ago because the music was too loud. Before hopping off the barstool and heading for the corridor.

Tetchy saw Juliet Saramago kissing another girl and thought nothing of it. He only glimpsed Juliette Marquez when he made the first pass and did a double take. In what world would Juliet and Juliette hook up? He then resolved to investigate further.

"What the fuck!" Tetchy shouted, ripping Juliet and Juliette apart.

Juliette Marquez wiped her mouth and pushed Tetchy. "What do you mean, what the fuck? Mind your business, asshole."

Tetchy aimed a finger at Juliette Marquez's face. "You don't belong here?"

"Chill, I'm leaving."

"No!" Juliet grabbed her arm. "Don't go."

Juliet Saramago shoved Tetchy and gave him a deadly look. "You're drunk! You're a total dick, you know that? Just go home."

Tetchy staggered backward. But somehow shoved Juliet Saramago against the wall. Causing the plaster to crack. He wiped his sleeve as though Juliet had soiled him with her hands. "You stupid bitch, this is blunder beetle silk." He eyed Juliet as she plummeted to the stone floor. "You have no loyalty kissing that disgusting blabber hoof."

Juliette Marquez gasped and hoisted Juliet from the floor. "Fucking asshole!"

Her lip trickled blood. Juliet's face must have hit the wall on impact. "I'm okay."

"You're bleeding."

She touched her lip and looked at the blood on her fingertip. Her hands trembled. "Is it bad?" She said, while staring into Juliette Marquez's eyes.

Tetchy had busted her lip pretty good. From the sight of it, the cut went deep. Juliette Marquez saw nothing but fire after that. And punched Tetchy in the face as hard as she could. The powerful blow knocked Techy backward. He landed on a spider wood console table, causing everything to shatter to the floor.

Juliette Marquez screamed, "I'll punch your clock if you ever touch her again!"

* * *

Devin had crashed the rager alongside Juliette and a few others from the House of Marquez. Devin was drunk and unmasked, partying with Tetchy before the fight with Juliette started.

Despite the deadly feud between the houses, nobody seemed to care that Devin had crashed the party. They had even cheered when Devin made his big revelation. Chanting "Devin, Devin, Devin" as he dirty danced to music with Veronica and Lindsay.

Regardless of which house he belonged to, everyone in the land loved Devin. But he was still Marquez stock. And would be the first person implicated if anything nefarious should arise from a night of partying. Say, for example, a dead body.

Juliet screamed when Juliette Marquez stooped to check on her. Juliette Marquez saw utter fear oozing from Juliet's face and knew something was wrong. "Who the fuck do you think you are?"

Tetchy aimed a gun at the back of Juliette Marquez's head. "Chill, bro." Juliette Marquez pointed to Juliet's bloody lip. "Look what you did."

"I said, who the fuck do you think you are?" Juliette Marquez held out her hands.

"Don't!"

Tetchy closed in and pointed the gun at her nose. The gun's sensor screamed to life. "Tell your girlfriend to shut the fuck up."

Juliet Saramago jumped between the two. "Leave, now!" She pointed toward the front door.

Tetchy smiled, then raised the gun as though he meant to strike

Juliet down. When Juliet braced for impact, Juliette Marquez yanked her out of harm's way and reached for the gun.

A struggle ensued. The gun discharged. The gunshot thundered in the corridor like a high-speed train. A wisp of gunpowder smoke danced toward the ceiling. Juliet Saramago screamed, "Juliette!"

Tetchy and Juliette locked eyes. His lips twitched. He couldn't decide if pleasure or pain had landed. Then he collapsed on the floor. Juliette looked at Tetchy and saw his blood on her hands.

"You're bleeding," Juliet Saramago said. Her shaky hands examined Juliette to see where the blood was coming.

"It's not me," Juliette Marquez said, staring down at Tetchy's lifeless body.

A partygoer wearing all black stumbled upon the bloody scene and screamed.

Juliet Saramago kissed Juliette Marquez and said, "You have to leave."

Juliette Marquez gleamed with confliction, as though fear and love couldn't dwell in the same space. "It was an accident."

"They'll never believe that." Juliet's eyes looked frightened. "Do you love me?"

Juliette Marquez took a few steps back and nodded.

"Then meet me at Sacred Arch."

"What?"

"If we wed," her desperate tone sent shivers through Juliette Marquez, "they can't touch us."

Another partygoer screamed in the distance. Juliette Marquez kissed Juliet. She hesitated to leave. In her mind, a longer stay trumped a return to a lifetime of emptiness. They absorbed each other with their eyes.

Juliet didn't want to spend another second without Juliette Marquez. But she knew Juliette Marquez's life was in danger. The House of Saramago would kill her. "Go." Her voice was still shaky. "They'll punch your clock."

Unbeknownst to Juliet and Juliette, someone had been watching the whole thing go down at the end of the corridor. After Devin had made out with Lindsay in the bathroom and was heading back to the ballroom to schmooze Veronica. He overheard the argument and then the gunshot. He saw Tetchy crumble to the floor. But more damning than that. He saw Juliette Marquez hovering over the body with a gun in hand. From his vantage point, he didn't see Juliet Saramago standing off to the side. He saw Juliette Marquez talking to someone. But who, he couldn't say.

Four by Day & Two Shall Live

Everything in Mafia Land is stuck in a loop. What serves a purpose initially fades away and finds its way back. Unlike all things in life, some things that return don't always receive a smile. As if to say, righting sins of the past comes at a price.

This story serves as the record. It shall be no different. And mirrors the daily lives of everyone in the universe. Regardless of which planet.

Mother Saramago and Mother Marquez rushed to Leonor's bedside. Not because they cared whether she lived or died. They feared the end of Mafia Land. But more to the point, they feared the return of Land of Kings. Something that could set women back another twenty-five thousand years.

A near-death experience couldn't wipe a lifetime of a sneer from Leonor's face. She was stuck in a perpetual sneer. A frightful gaze. Something crafted over the years.

"Leonor." Mother Saramago got straight to the point. Using the devil may care attitude. "You must stop this at once. This has gone to the poodle gnats."

Leonor glared at Mother Saramago. Then Mother Marquez. Mother Marquez broke eye contact out of fear. Leonor could slice

Mother Marquez's throat with those predator eyes. "I had every right to protect myself. Mother Carlito stabbed me first. What else could I do?"

That damn little, teeny, tiny voice Leonor used. It dug underneath Mother Saramago's skin like a hot poker. That childlike tone was nothing more than a gimmick. She knew it. They knew it. Everybody knew it. Mother Saramago has no desire to play along. "Well, there you have it. We can put this mess behind us."

"No." Leonor raised the top half of the bed to gain a better view. The bed hummed and settled at a right angle. "The law states I may challenge Mother Carlito and Frida. Blood in, blood out."

"You cannot challenge a Mother, dear girl," Mother Marquez said. "You no longer have oath on your side."

Leonor giggled, then halted and clung to her bandaged hip. Those drugs fucked her mind. She wasn't thinking clear enough.

"You see," Mother Saramago pointed, "you are in no shape to fight for your life."

"I guess Uncle was mistaken." Leonor gritted her teeth and lowered the bed to reduce the pressure building in her hip. "You're not that smart."

"Careful, Leonor."

"What more can you take from me?"

"Why did you lie about being pregnant," Mother Marquez's voice rose from behind. She stepped a few feet closer.

"Freedom comes at a price. Your Mother understood that." Mother Saramago held her back, overriding Mother Marquez's question. "We cannot take responsibility for what Stigmata did."

Leonor ignored Mother Marquez. And counted her fingers. "First, I'll kill Frida. Then Mother Carlito. Then I'll kill you two. I'll be the only Mother left in Mafia Land."

Mother Marquez hiked her fists, ready to swing. "Come on, girl. Let's see what you've got. I have nothing to lose."

Leonor put on a fake scared face and shriveled. Using a childish voice, she said, "Oh, no. Please don't hurt me, boomer," then giggled.

Mother Marquez sprang into action and took a swing. Mother

Saramago yanked Mother Marquez off Leonor. "Stop!" She pushed Mother Marquez further back. "Can't you see what she's doing? She wants to gain oath on a technicality."

"I guess Uncle was right after all," Leonor said with that girly voice as she spewed another sinister giggle.

"You'll die in the arena." Mother Saramago's voice was ferocious. "I'll see to that."

Leonor shriveled up again. Contorted her arms and hands, as though she were a helpless animal. "I hope you do a better job than you did with Juliet."

Mother Saramago appeared as though she wanted to slap the hell out of Leonor. But somehow dialed down the rage.

Mother Marquez jumped between the two and pointed a damning finger. "Why do you risk your life for that man?"

Leonor glared at Mother Marquez like she had hit a nerve.

"He doesn't love you. Men like that don't love."

"Have you seen Jinx around lately?"

Mother Saramago seemed stunned. Mother Marquez scrutinized Mother Saramago, curious to know what Leonor was talking about.

"Check the greenhouse. I hear flowers mask the scent of death."

"What is she talking about?"

"Yeah," Leonor taunted, "we'd all like to know."

"Nothing." Mother Saramago shook her head with that haunting look aimed at Leonor. "You gain nothing by doing this."

"What is she talking about?" Mother Marquez locked eyes on Mother Saramago.

"I won't say it in front of her."

Mother Saramago peered down at Leonor. "You're too young to remember what women endured. We have endured. We'll survive you too." Mother Saramago walked out of the room and left Mother Marquez behind to deal with the aftermath.

"I can respect what you've done," Mother Marquez said. "But what I won't respect is you doing all this for a man. He's using you because he can't win. You'll lose just like he did."

Leonor said nothing. Her eyes were as glossy as jewels. Her sneer conveyed the rest.

* * *

Mother Marquez followed Mother Saramago as she charged down the hall. She didn't know where Mother Saramago was going. But soon realized she was heading toward Mother Carlito's hospital room.

Mother Saramago got straight to the point when she laid eyes on Mother Carlito. "You have no choice. You must fight Leonor in the arena."

Mother Carlito looked a little helpless in that infirmary bed and grabbed her throat. "How?" she said, as though she were talking through a tin can.

"You and Frida must join forces. It's the only way," Mother Saramago said as panic set in. "Is Frida prepared?"

"Mothers enforce oath. We don't take part," Mother Marquez said, out of breath. "We have the power to change the rules."

Mother Saramago turned to face Mother Marquez. "That's exactly what they want."

"That's what who wants?"

"Stigmata and Leonor. Don't underestimate the power of Tories." Mother Saramago stepped closer. Almost nose to nose. "If we manipulate the laws, then we're no better. Then," Mother turned to face Mother Carlito, "things will go back to the way they were."

"A Mother title should suffice, don't you think?"

Mother Saramago gave a look of disbelief. "Leonor has been playing us since the beginning. She wants us to believe she has a desire to be Mother. When, in reality, she wants to destroy Mafia Land."

"What… should…we…do?" Mother Carlito clung to that sutured throat.

Mother Saramago peered down at Mother Carlito, then Mother Marquez. "We do what we've always done—we outplay. No one knows the game better than us." Mother Saramago edged closer to Mother Carlito's bedside. "Stigmata and Leonor played their cards too soon. Don't forget what hangs in the balance. Girls can now study science and mathematics. Your niece is in medical school." She turned to face Mother Marquez. "Your niece will be the first woman in space. Our lives aren't more valuable than what we've built."

Mother Carlito cackled in agony. "The irony… a…girl wants to destroy…a land…for women." Mother Carlito stared at Mother Marquez. Then Mother Saramago. "I…give…my life…" She was out of breath and pointed at both to finish her sentence.

Mother Marquez glanced at Mother Saramago. "We can't all die. Who will lead Mafia Land?" She closed her eyes and muttered to herself.

"Our rule was a temporary solution until we created a viable democracy. But we got complacent. We must pay the price." Mother Saramago glanced at Mother Carlito.

"She's…right."

"Then we right wrongs, starting today." Mother Marquez rubbed her hands together. "How do we destroy Leonor?"

"We must strike now," Mother Saramago paced, "while Leonor is weak. You have a better chance of killing her before she regains her strength."

"Fight for life isn't until tomorrow."

"You must strike now. We don't want to give her any more time to recuperate."

"What about Stigmata?"

"Oh, I wouldn't concern yourself with him," Mother Saramago said. "It's being handled."

* * *

The moment Juliet kissed Juliette Marquez. After that fateful night. Where a bullet ricocheted past Tetchy's rib cage and pierced the heart. As fate would have it. They were inseparable. Not in the physical sense, as one would hope, rather an emotional sense. A connection of the mind. Which leads to the heart.

Contrary to popular belief, hearts can, and do, grow fonder in the digital world, like bacteria in a petri dish. The human heart can make do with little. Or live on fumes, if one is so inclined. Human touch is not always required when building love, one story at a time. Fascination and a pinch of mystery are all it takes to brew a love spell. Juliet found Juliette Marquez to be all these things—and then some.

A passionate digital relationship developed between the two in a matter of days. Spending hours texting each other. Sometimes all night long until every sun rose and fell. At least once. Or was it twice?

Juliet: devin saw u kill tetchy

Juliette: GR8

Juliet: don think like that

Juliette:

Juliet: What about sacred

Juliette: fight for life

Juliet: no way!!!

Juliette:

Juliet: do u love me

Juliette:

Juliet: Do u want to be with me

Juliette: fucking, of course!!! U?

Juliet: meet at sacred.

Juliette: (text bubble displays three rotating dots in perpetual spin.)

Juliet: yes or no

Juliette: i dont want u to get hurt

Juliet: hurt???

Juliette: not like that if they make u fight too

Juliet: they cant make us if we wed

Juliette: ok

Juliet: tomorrow at sacred

Juliet: k

Juliet: sister claude

Juliette Marquez: 😔

* * *

Mother Saramago peered up at the ceiling and could feel the crowd hammer in their seats. Even the walls swelled and vibrated from two levels below. The concrete and steel rebar construction became a clamorous drum. Somehow, that boom grew steady and louder each minute. Chants and cheers electrified the air and flooded the locker room.

Even though they prepared for battle two levels below, they could hear the cries for justice. The crowd's steady percussion rattled Mother Marquez's chest. Those chants and cheers seemed to swallow them. Outer space was not far enough to escape the arena.

Mother Marquez glided a sharpening stone across the blade.

"The turnout is surprising on such short notice," Mother Saramago said while wrapping Frida's forearm in athletic tape. "I don't recall the arena ever being this loud."

Mother Marquez gave a look. "It's always this loud. It was even louder when the state leaders entered the arena."

"I don't recall that." Mother Saramago looked up and stopped wrapping Frida's forearm. "It's been some time."

"Yes." Mother Marquez continued sharpening her sword. "Way louder."

"I guess I never realized how loud it really was at this vantage."

"Frida." Mother Carlito said. "Let…us," she pointed to Mother Marquez, "fight…Leonor…first. If we…fail…then you."

"She killed Königsmarck!" Frida's voice somehow drowned out the noise from the arena. "I won't sit back and watch. I want to see the look on her face when I drive my blade into her."

"Oh…blabber…hoof," Mother Carlito said.

Mother Marquez rolled her eyes and slid the blade into its sheath.

Mother Saramago ripped the tape from Frida's forearm, frustrated. "Leonor is a trained assassin. Get that through your head."

"So," Frida inspected her forearm, making sure the tape was tight enough against her skin, "I'm not scared of Leonor."

"Hear my words, girl." Mother Saramago snatched Frida's chin and yanked it upward so that Frida would lock eyes. "She's no common assassin. A sadistic monster trained her. Make no mistake. She is a monster. Don't give her an inch, or otherwise…"

"Otherwise, what?" Frida glared at Mother Carlito. "Why are you guys so damn scared? She's squad just like me."

"Frida," Mother Carlito strapped a dagger sheath to her thigh, "for… once, just…listen. If…we're scared," Mother Carlito panted, "you…should be…too."

"We should all attack at once." Mother Marquez laced athletic tap between her fingers. "Catch her off guard. Hack away." Mother Marquez swung the blade in the air with a hacking motion.

Frida gave a horrified look.

"Yes." Mother Carlito's eyes beamed. "A full…attack at…same time… I like…it." Mother Carlito peered at Mother Saramago, waiting for her input.

Mother Saramago glared at each of them with a worried look. "Yes." Mother Saramago walked over to the weapon case. Scanning the many swords, daggers, and spiked bludgeon balls. "That is expert advice for a layperson." Mother Saramago glared at each of them, "Leonor is Stigmata's pupil."

"What do you…suggest?" Mother Carlito clung to her throat in pain. "Raise…our hands high…in surrender? Let her…cut us down?"

"If we're to survive, we must outsmart her." Mother Saramago handed Frida a teeny aerosol spritzer. "There is no honor in the arena. Kick dirt in her face. Throw anything in arm's reach at her. Rip out her eyes if you can. Pin her down. Then, cut off her head."

Frida looked even more horrified. "What's this for?"

"It will blind her for a minute," Mother Saramago said with an evil tone. "Make sure you don't blind yourself."

"Fighting dirty was the old ways." Mother Marquez grabbed the aerosol spritzer from Frida's hand. "If we die, we die with oath. That's tradition. Otherwise, we're no better."

Mother Carlito chuckled, still holding her throat. "Land of… Kings." Mother Carlito strapped a smaller sheath to her ankle. "If… Leonor wins…oath, Mafia…Land…will fall. We all…know what…that means." She walked over to Mother Marquez and opened her hand. "Give me…the spritzer. The old…ways…never left."

* * *

Mother Saramago stood inside the media box and peered at the energetic crowd. "As I stand before you, citizens of Mafia Land," Mother Saramago said, raising her hand.

The crowd hushed to murmurs and whispers, awaiting her address.

"Mafia Land is under attack by one of our own, Leonor Saramago."

The crowd's boos and foot stomps quaked the ground.

"Today," the microphone digitized Mother Saramago's voice. A robotic tone stung the ears of the crowd. "Two Mothers will fight together for the first time, alongside Frida Carlito."

The crowd cheered.

"Their titles are being challenged by Leonor."

Jeers and boos caused a deafening stir.

Mother Saramago feathered her hands to silence the crowd.

"There is a dark force among you. It wants to destroy Mafia Land. Today we defeat that dark force. You will have your justice!"

The arena gates crept open. Leonor sauntered onto the field and stabbed the air with her sword. Each opposition had a microphone to talk to the crowd. Some used the platform to plead their case. While others went into that good dirt.

Leonor ripped the microphone from the stand. "Nothing but lies spill from the Mothers." She aimed her sword at Mother Carlito, as they walked onto the field. "I challenge their oath."

The crowd fell silent.

"If Mafia Land is being consumed by dark forces," Leonor looked at the crowd, steely eyed, "look no further than the Mothers. Today, I will rid the land of oppression. No more kings. No queens."

The crowd was quiet at first. Enough to hear a blunder beetle snap its wings. As the seconds crept along, the crowd erupted. One by one, the crowd rose to their feet.

Mother Carlito snatched the microphone to denounce Leonor's speech, though her puny voice was no match for the cheering spectators. Mother Marquez pulled Mother Carlito back, so she wouldn't humiliate herself any further.

Frida locked eyes on Leonor. Somewhere below, the pain of lost love, or maybe longing, struck an evil chord inside. Inward pain turns to anger. When anger no longer satisfies, evil takes its rightful place. And sits at the right hand of a long table. That's when evil became her.

Leonor was about to say more when Frida whipped her arm back and hurled a golden spear that raced toward Leonor. The golden spear sliced her cheek as it whizzed past and slammed into the perimeter wall with a thud. The sound of metal striking wood made the handle dong.

The bloodthirsty crowd cheered.

Mother Carlito screamed, "Frida!"

Leonor and Frida charged each other at full tilt. Letting their swords navigate their deadly course. "Blood in, blood out," Frida whispered as the dirt smoke rose from her feet.

Mother Carlito and Mother Marquez sprang into action and

darted after Frida. Frida swung her blade wildly, trying to remove Leonor's head, but hit nothing. Leonor sidestepped, avoiding the blade's razor edge.

Frida backed away and swung again. This time, Leonor deflected the blow. Steel smashed against steel. Sparks and a high-pitched clang echoed.

"I only want the Mothers," Leonor said, panting. It took everything she had to hold Frida back. The mighty punch that Frida packed beneath her petite, elegant frame, which harkened back to the old world, surprised.

"I loved him!" Frida's eyes burned like stars in the sky. Yet the tears were not far behind. "You killed Königsmarck, bitch!" Frida slammed the blade into Leonor's calf. Leonor's flesh gaped wide and oozed blood.

Leonor winced in agony and swung the sword upward and clipped Frida's chin. A trail of blood sailed skyward. Frida didn't even flinch. She knew no pain like love lost. Love stripped from her fingertips. She went for Leonor's throat yet again and jabbed for the jugular.

Frida spun that steel around, never stumbling. Beating Leonor down with everything she had. Never giving a moment's rest. All Leonor can do was to counter the attack. From a distance, the arena was a mountain of clinging steel and sparks. For the first time since they hatched the plan, Leonor's eyes showed fear. Frida's sheer force wore Leonor down to nothing.

"Move out...of the...way," Mother Carlito told Frida as she threw a spear at Leonor. The spear narrowly missed Leonor and sailed into the dirt. Mother Carlito was slower and didn't have the strength of her daughter.

Mother Marquez charged Leonor, dagger in hand, and aimed for Leonor's gut. She hit flesh or something. But Mother Marquez couldn't see where the dagger had landed.

Anger had Frida. The sword battle tangled the girls with only one outcome. The Mothers couldn't seem to kill Leonor without killing Frida.

Unbeknownst to Mother Marquez, her dagger had pierced Frida's ribcage. Not Leonor, as she had hoped. Mother Carlito grabbed Leonor from behind and wrapped her arm around her neck. Mother Carlito squeezed as tight as she could to strangle Leonor and end the madness.

Leonor squirmed free, sidestepped the tangled mess of bodies, and rammed her sword behind her, hitting Mother Carlito. Mother Marquez saw the blade enter Mother Carlito and dug her nails into Leonor's bandaged wound.

The crowd was cinematic. The only thing that could satisfy was blood. Their cries electrified the air. Steady chants charged toward the sky. Spectators on the left side of the arena pounded their feet.

"Kill her, Frida." A person's voice broke through the sound barrier.

Leonor screamed. Tears spouted. Frida stopped swinging her sword once Mother Carlito sank to the floor. Mother Carlito was wearing a strange look as blood gushed from her hands. She stared up at the sky while her shirt turned bright red. Frida didn't realize she could have won had she kept pummeling Leonor. The moment Frida stopped to check on Mother Carlito, Leonor regained momentum.

With a powerful blow, Leonor ripped free. And beheaded Mother Marquez in one elegant, sweeping motion. A bloody stream spiraled through the air. And Mother Marquez crumbled to the floor. That headless body lay twitching in the dirt as though her brain were still working.

The crowd quieted.

A woman stood, pointed at Leonor, and screamed, "She killed Mother Marquez!"

Leonor peered at Frida as she kneeled beside Mother Carlito, clinging to her hand. The time had passed. Mother Carlito was gone.

With Frida's back turned, Leonor raised her sword to strike her.

"Coward!" someone shouted.

A few people in the crowed stood, hands covering their mouth.

"You don't deserve oath!"

Leonor studied the crowd with careful inspection. Tears formed in her eyes. The plan went awry. Leonor thought Mafia Land would embrace her. Would embrace new ideas. Not from kings and queens.

Not like Seneca, but something else. A forward world. Seneca's technological advances were fools' platinum. Still governed in the old ways. Still harboring an ancient mindset.

No, Leonor wanted a world free of death notes. And death dealings. And prisons. And oaths. And the arena. And bureaucratic hogwash. Not a path handed down by oligarchs. As it stood, Mafia Land didn't have an endless supply of bodies to keep the fire stoked. Eventually, they would run out of bodies.

Mother Saramago could not hide the heartbreak. Her eyes glistened with tears. She stood in the media booth with a hand over her chest. Leonor hurled her weapon at the dirt and displayed bloody hands for the crowd to see. "These bloody hands belong to you, Mafia Land." She grabbed Frida's shoulder. "This ends now."

Frida jerked free and peered up at Leonor. Tears streaked her dusty face. "You took everything from me."

Leonor didn't answer.

Frida gave Leonor a look of shock. Or a look of ultimate betrayal, perhaps. "How could you do this?"

A person in the crowd shouted, "They freed us!"

"Remember what it was like before?" Frida said.

Leonor stayed silent and just stared at Frida.

"Answer me!" Frida collapsed onto Mother Carlito and sobbed.

"Traitor!" A spectator shouted.

Leonor could not bear the weight of Frida's pain. Often, the eyes first translate heartbreak. Then the body. From one heartbreak to the next. One knows the look of heartbreak. Though, foremost, Frida's heartbroken eyes belonged to Leonor.

"Punch her clock, Mother Saramago!" Someone stood and screamed.

"Deny oath!" Another in the crowd demanded.

Leonor backed away from Frida and headed toward the arena gate. A composite bottle struck Leonor's foot. A sloth tomato splattered her face. The gooey insides dripped down her neck. Then a tidal wave of trash came flying.

"Stop!" Mother Saramago screamed into the microphone. Her

voice echoed through the arena. "Leonor has earned oath. Like it or not. That is tradition."

"Traitor!"

More spectators booed. The crowd rumbled like a stampede of blabber hoofs.

Mother Saramago raised her hands. "We must honor oath if we are to continue Mafia Land."

"Deny oath!"

"If I deny Leonor oath, then I would deny your right. Or anyone else." Mother Saramago pointed to the sky. "Leonor doesn't deserve oath. Nevertheless, she has earned it."

"I will never serve Leonor!" A woman stood.

The audience wouldn't be appeased until they drained every drop of blood from Leonor.

Uncle Stigmata 3.0

MOTHER SARAMAGO WENT to the arena lounge where Leonor sat, nursing her wounds and drinking fig bubbles at the smart bar. Mother placed a large dagger on the counter and slid it over.

"What's this?"

"My daughter is dead. My best friends are dead. You might as well finish the job." Mother Saramago stood, arms at her sides. "You're at the precipice. Finish what you started."

Leonor slid the dagger back over. "I thought it would feel better than this." She looked like a wounded child, crying in her blabber hoof milk.

"Now you know the burden."

"What now?" Leonor sniffled. "Death note?"

"No." Mother Saramago sat at the smart bar. A hologram sparked to life. "Fig bubbles and platinum elixir." Mother Saramago glared at Leonor. "It's your choice, Leonor. It always was."

"I have to finish it." Leonor didn't make eye contact. She kept staring into her glass. Twisting a bar napkin around her fingers.

"What are you waiting for."

"I never wanted to punch your clock. I only wanted Mother Carlito."

Mother Saramago's voice rose. "What did she do to deserve this?"

"She betrayed father and mother."

Mother Saramago rubbed her temples, as though a headache was settling in. "I imagine Stigmata convinced you of such things."

"Uncle Stigmata is shady. I knew that. I found the state leader who murdered my parents. I tortured him until he confessed."

Mother Saramago looked intrigued and leaned closer. "You know as well as I, you can never trust what someone says while on the hook."

"Mother Carlito threw my parents to the poodle gnats." Leonor was crying. "They were going to hang her for smuggling holograms out of the state virtual library, and then she gave everyone up to spare her life."

"That's how the deep state found out?" Mother Saramago's eyes went wide. She covered her mouth. "Why didn't I see that."

Leonor nodded.

"Why would Stigmata allow you to poke around in deep state records?" Mother Saramago's intrigue hit the ceiling while she sipped fig bubbles and guzzled platinum elixir.

"I made him think I'd die for the cause." Leonor traced a finger around the wet ring on her cocktail napkin. "But I was just using him to find out who killed my parents. He's the last person on my list."

Mother Saramago put down her drink. "I wouldn't worry about Stigmata. Remedios is taking care of him as we speak."

Leonor's eye lit up, and she looked at Mother Saramago. "It's a trap. Seneca is protecting Uncle Stigmata."

"One cannot erase every sin, Leonor. But now is the time to try. Before it's too late."

* * *

After the blue sensor scanned her face, a guard escorted Remedios to the seventh floor. Someone had already positioned a chair in front of the parking space.

Stigmata sat facing that empty chair, as though he were expecting her any second. His manicured appearance was a stark contrast to when they had first met. He held out his hand, still wearing that disturbing smile. "Have a seat, dear child. I imagine you're weary from your travels."

Remedios settled in and kept her eyes fixed on Stigmata. At the corner of her eye, she saw a guard edge closer. "How'd you know I'd be here?"

"Oh, a little zigzag whispered in my ear."

"La, la, la, la." The guard reached for Remedios. But she kicked the chair out from under her and punched his jugular. The guard crashed to the floor, choking on his own tongue.

"Impressive, dear child. Very impressive. You have the heart of an assassin. Now finish him."

Remedios kneeled and injected the guard with something. Stigmata couldn't see the substance. He smeared his face against the energy shield and went tippy-toe to gain a better picture. "Smart girl, but you cannot stop them all."

"La, la, la, la."

Stigmata hammered the energy shield with his knuckles. "Are we forgetting something, child?"

Remedios fished a tiny device from her waistband and aimed it at the control panel. The energy shield digitized from the floor with a thunderous gear sound.

"What a lovely contraption." Stigmata's eyes sparkled. His creepy smile never faltered.

Remedios sprinted to the elevator and pointed the device at the digital panel. The alarm sounded. Then blue strobes ignited the seventh floor.

The energy shield was slow to dissolve. Remedios watched Stigmata while the energy shield receded toward the ceiling. The mechanism produced a steady hum.

"I think you've done it now. They'll certainly kill you where you stand."

"They won't make it in time."

Stigmata rolled his eyes. "Girls are very good assassins. But you haven't thought it through. Even a blabber hoof can see that."

Remedios fished more gadgets from her waistband. "La, la, la, la, la."

"You come prepared, and that is key."

Remedios darted to the panoramic windows and chucked a gooey substance against the glass. As the energy shield receded, a horrible smell wafted from the cell, as though breaking the seal of a crypt. Remedios covered her nose with her sleeve. "Don't they give you showers?"

Stigmata shrugged. "Vanity isn't everything."

When the energy shield finally vanished and Remedios heard the mechanism lock in place with a clunk, she flailed her hands. "Well, aren't you going to run or something?"

"I would, child, but I have a dodgy ankle. I couldn't make it if I tried."

"Really? You're going to make me work for it?" Remedios reached for Stigmata and landed on her ass. She beamed a look of bewilderment and peered at him.

"Oh, you disappoint. I had such high hopes."

Remedios sprung to her feet and bum-rushed Stigmata. Stigmata moved swiftly, diverting all her weight to go the opposite direction. She skidded across the floor face-first. When she landed, a loud grunt spewed, as though she had the wind knocked out of her.

Remedios rose and removed more gadgets from her pocket. She speedily assembled something in her hand.

"What are you doing now, child? The fight hasn't even begun."

Within in seconds, she had assembled a gun. She cocked the composite contraption with a click and aimed the barrel at Stigmata. "I'm just going to fucking shoot you boomer style."

"Boomer." Stigmata's voice shrieked. "What do they teach you in Mafia Land?"

Remedios fired the gun. The bullet slammed into Stigmata, spinning him backward. But it didn't take him down. He regained his posture and walked toward Remedios. Her hands were shaky as hell.

She tried loading another bullet. But it slipped from her grip and hit the floor with a tink. She panicked and reached for another bullet. Though Stigmata was already upon her. He swept her feet out from under. She smacked her head on the concrete floor. Her world spun. Her eyes darted in circles, unable to focus. "What the fuck?"

Stigmata lifted his shirt. "Bulletproof."

He smashed Remedios' face with his foot, knocking her unconscious.

* * *

Leonor noticed a guard stationed at the elevator door once she entered Seneca Corrections Institute. No guard manned the energy shield window. That gave her gut a real twist. Remedios was her BFF. And she feared the worst. Her mind raced faster than her body would allow. She limped past the energy shield window and toward the elevator. Frida had done a real number on her because the gash on her leg was bloody and burning like hell.

"Where's the guard?" Leonor pointed back at that energy shield window as she winced. She clutched her hip in pain. "I need to see Stigmata."

The guard held out her hand. Stopping Leonor from coming any closer. "The building is in lockdown. You'll have to come back tomorrow."

The indicator panel above the elevator door blazed. Every single floor. But the seventh floor was blinking red. She had never seen digital red before. Under any circumstance. Anything digital in Mafia Land was blue or amber. "Is the seventh floor on fire?"

The guard peered up at the indicator panel with nonchalant eyes. "Someone tripped the alarm on the seven floor. That's why the building is on lockdown."

"Tripped?" Leonor clung to her injured leg. "Like someone's trying to escape?"

The guard didn't seem amused by Leonor's choice of words. "Like I said."

Leonor yanked a gun from her side and aimed the barrel at the guard's head. "You're going to get me to the seventh floor."

The guard winced and raised her twitchy hands. "Don't shoot."

Leonor used the gun like a laser pointer and aimed the barrel at the guard's holster. "You ever kill anyone with that thing?"

"It's an energy gun." Tears slid down the guard's cheeks.

"Have you ever watched someone die?"

The guard shook her head, then made a face. "My grandma, I guess."

"My body count will give you nightmares."

The guard gulped hard with the look of death scribbled on her face.

"You'd make a tiny splash. Understand."

"You can't reach the seventh floor by elevator."

"Why not?"

"The building is on lockdown." Her teeth rattled.

Leonor pressed the barrel against the guard's forehead and armed the trigger. The gun sensor chimed a whir. "One...two."

The guard trembled. She pointed down a long corridor. "I can get into the stairwell. But you need a keycard to access the seventh floor."

"You don't have access?"

The guard shook her head, squeezing her eyes shut. "Please, don't shoot."

Leonor smiled that crazy, sadistic smile. "Get me to the seventh floor, or I'll blow a hole right through that pretty little skull. Get it?"

The guard eagerly nodded and pointed. "The guard station has an override."

"Really?" Leonor sounded flabbergasted. "I just told you my body count. Does nothing move you?"

"Sorry." The guard cowered, as though preparing for Leonor to blow her brains out.

"You know what?" Leonor raised the gun high. "Your grandma deserved better." And bashed the guard's nose with the butt of the gun, causing her to sail to the floor. Leonor ripped the keycard from the guard's shirt pocket and headed for the guard station.

She limped and agonized over each step. The climb was slow and arduous. It gave her time to analyze the situation. Uncle Stigmata's voice ringing at the back of her head. Making her go crazy and paranoid. Piercing red strobes exploded everywhere the moment she opened the seventh floor door. Her entire body was now pulsing laser red. It seemed the laser tunneled through her body. That hip and leg burned.

In the distance, she saw two guards lying unconscious near the crop of prisoners. More guards lay unconscious along the way as she headed for Uncle Stigmata. The seventh floor was silent, even though the strobe lights were burning in the backdrop. As though someone had killed all the sound the world could muster.

Each blue, square outline she passed held a prisoner in suspension like a department-store mannequin. A permanent macabre pose froze men and women of all ages.

That laser red strobe breathed new life into those dead eyes that gazed out of the invisible box and into the nothingness. Their mouths agape. As though the freezing process didn't give them enough time to shut that trap. What they were staring toward, Leonor did not know. Maybe stuck in an artificial dreamworld.

But as she looked on, as far as the eye could see, those red strobes lent optical illusion to the field of invisible boxes. The light was so powerful that when it glided across the suspended prisoners; it appeared as though they were being burned alive. No longer a crop, but a field of burning bodies.

As Leonor drew closer, she saw Uncle Stigmata's invisible box empty. He was no longer limited to the energy shield. Remedios was lying unconscious a few feet from the blue outline. Leonor tracked Uncle Stigmata as she stooped to check Remedios's pulse.

"She's still alive, my child, I assure you." Uncle Stigmata's back was turned. He scribbled something down at the desk. "Think of her as leftovers. Like a glass-newt dinner."

"Get up." Leonor pointed her gun at Uncle Stigmata. Her bandaged leg was sopping in blood. "Slowly."

He turned to face Leonor. Annoyance engraved on his face. "An assassin of your talent knows the probability of landing a shot."

"I just got my ass beat in the arena, so don't give me any shit."

"You've never disappointed me before, dear child," Uncle Stigmata raised a finger, "except for today."

"You're the last," she said. "Then it's finished."

"Finished?" Uncle Stigmata said, as though he could not believe that word had escaped her mouth. He stretched his hand out. "You're my greatest creation, Leonor. You inspire me and terrorize. That's why this will never be over."

"You created a monster!" Leonor armed the trigger, causing the sensor to rev to a high-pitched chime.

"Monster." Uncle Stigmata sounded insulted and placed a hand over his heart. He pointed at Leonor. "Look around. This existence is an illusion. Can't you see? I taught you how to think for yourself. Pride and corruption has infected this world. It's unredeemable. It must burn. And you are going to light the match."

"What about Land of Kings?" Leonor waved the gun around. "That's what you wanted."

"I taught you to think bigger, Leonor." Stigmata flicked his hand. "I lead you right to the party leaders. You did as I suspected and killed everyone. Including the Founder. I laughed when I heard you murdered Charles. You know how I get. Sometimes I can't hold back the emotions. I knew it was you. Come on," he raised his voice for effect, "we all knew it was you. Even Salvador. Then you moved on to the Mothers. That one touched me. That one *really touched* me. You are free of this world, Leonor. You destroyed Mafia Land. Seneca too. You did what no one else could." Uncle Stigmata wiped his eyes.

"Are you crying?"

"Dear child," Uncle Stigmata glared, "You can create something good." Uncle Stigmata raised his hands toward the ceiling. "Do what you came to do. Finish what you've started." Uncle Stigmata closed his eyes and tilted his face upward. "You no longer require wisdom from an old man."

Leonor aimed the gun at Uncle Stigmata. The gun rattled in her grip. Leonor squeezed the gun handle so tight. Imagining it was Uncle Stigmata's throat instead. Her eyes watery. Her vision blurred. "Why?" Leonor's voice quivered. "You destroyed everything I loved."

"Time is running out, dear child." Uncle Stigmata ignored the question, neck cocked. Still glistening in strobe light. Face pointing to the rafters. "The guards will storm the seventh floor any second."

The gun stopped rattling. Leonor lowered it to her side. "I hate you for what you've done. But I still love you." Leonor kneeled down and tried to revive Remedios.

"Shoot!" Uncle Stigmata erupted. "I did this for you. For Remedios. Maybe not her. But certainly for you. Sometimes you must burn the village to the ground to create a better world." His eyes wildly searched the room. He rummaged his brain for the right words. "My death will usher a true beginning."

Uncle Stigmata always knew what to say. Except for today. Whatever arrogance or pride or snootiness he had brandished in the outside world had withered over the years. He was stripped down to the veins inside the invisible box. To reveal something human. Something good. Despite the evil carnage.

Leonor helped Remedios to her feet and faced Uncle Stigmata. At first, she mouthed *love*. But no words came out. She paused, then closed her mouth.

"Don't just stand there, shoot!"

Leonor put the gun on the floor and kicked it over to Uncle Stigmata.

"I taught you to kill the witness. They always come back to haunt." Uncle Stigmata was beside himself. The anger consuming him to the brink of disaster. He pointed a damning finger at Leonor. "It's an act of faith, you must be the one to do it."

Leonor and Remedios headed for the stairwell. They could still hear Uncle Stigmata blabbing.

Stigmata grabbed the gun. It whirred to a high-pitch. He pressed it against his temple. "Love is much like the truth, Leonor." That was that.

* * *

Leonor helped Remedios down the first flight of stairs.

"This doesn't make us even, you know?" Remedios said, using Leonor's shoulder as a crutch.

"Same."

Remedios was panting as they came upon the fifth floor. "Why didn't you punch his clock?"

"I'm done punching clocks."

Remedios stopped on the landing and gave Leonor a serious look. "Me too."

"Done with death dealing," they said.

"Your uncle can beat some ass. I mean, *really* beat some ass."

Leonor nodded. Her eyes were more focused on each step they took. "We're almost there."

"We're never goanna make it one step at a time." Remedios paused. "Just leave me."

"I'm not leaving you," Leonor said in a tone that suggested it should be obvious. "I got you into this."

"Touchy-feely is not your thing."

Leonor stayed quiet.

Before they reached the lobby, Remedios paused again. Sweat forming on her temples. They could hear a thousand boots trampling the ground. Like an army was assembling just beyond the door. She raised her gun. "I spoke too soon. No more death dealing after tonight."

"I told you, I'm done with that."

"Do you want to spend an eternity inside a box like all those zombies freaks upstairs?"

"Not really." Leonor fluttered her eyes.

"Are you sure? Because I distinctly remember there being a vacant box right next to Stigmata."

Leonor gave Remedios a dirty look.

"I'm just saying."

"Yeah," Leonor said. "You're always *just saying*."

"Facts, Leonor."

Before they exited the stairwell that led to the lobby, Remedios placed her ear on the steel door, hoping to scope out the situation.

"Do you hear anything?"

Remedios peered at Leonor and whispered, "It's too fucking quiet."

One by one, their weapons chimed.

"I'll go first," Leonor said.

Remedios yanked her back. "You're hobbling worse than me." She pushed Leonor out of the way. "Me first, then you."

Leonor rolled her eyes. "Does it really matter?"

"Yeah." Remedios quietly cracked open the door. "You might accidentally shoot me?"

"Seriously, bruh?" Leonor's voice rose. "That only happened, like, one time." Leonor raised a forefinger in Remedios's face. "*One time.*"

"Yeah, well," Remedios scoped out the lobby through the crack of the door, "I'm just saying, girl."

Leonor opened the door a little wider.

"Wait."

"What?"

"You and Tetchy." Remedios motioned with her hands. "Soulmates, or just cas?"

Leonor's eyes gave away the answer. When Remedios had mentioned Tetchy's name, it was as though Leonor had seen the ghost of him walk past.

"Really?" Remedios puckered her face. "I mean, *really?*" Remedios chuckled.

"Are we doing this?"

"Yeah." Remedios stopped laughing. "I just," she waved her hand as though the laugh were too painful.

"I lied, okay." Leonor stopped whispering. "I used him. Tetchy was a terrible fuck boy."

Remedios placed a finger to her lips. "Shhh."

Remedios scrunched her brows with intensity looming in her eyes. "You're a total baddie, Leonor. If we get our clocks punched today," Remedios peeked through the opening of the door, "I want it to be you. I thought you were a little shady at first. But now it makes sense."

"We played it, didn't we?"

"Yeah, girl," Remedios opened the door wide, "just saying."

* * *

The second Leonor and Remedios exited the stairwell, a slew of armed guards shouted, "Drop your weapons!" Gun sensors, one by one, screamed a thunderous whir. "Now!"

The guards had barricaded the main exit with energy shield walls. And from the looks of it, at least twenty-five strong pointed guns at Leonor and Remedios's heads.

Leonor glanced at Remedios, seeming to read her mind. As if she had the power to. Remedios shrugged.

"Drop your weapons!" The guard's tone thundered against concrete and glass and steel.

They locked eyes for a moment.

"We got this," Leonor said.

Remedios nodded. She aimed her gun at a guard. "I'm just glad it's you and no one else," she said, as though it could go either way. Still, she left the decision-making with Leonor.

"Do you want to end up in a box?"

"Nope." Remedios cracked her neck. "You?"

"I thought we talked about this a second ago." Leonor glanced at Remedios. But her focus remained on the guards ahead. "BFF, remember?"

"La, la, la, la." Remedios armed her weapon. The gun ominously ticked, poised to detonate. "Oh, shit. I almost forgot."

"Seriously, bruh?"

"We could have escaped from the seventh floor. I glued a sticky bomb to the window, right before Stigmata beat my ass."

Leonor glared at Remedios. She couldn't believe her ears. "We barely made it down seven flights of stairs, and now you mention the sticky bomb?"

Remedios smiled. "My bad. Should we try?"

A high-voltage bullet roared past them and exploded into a blue starburst against the concrete wall. "Final warning!"

"Their aim sucks." Remedios peered at Leonor. Face all compressed.

Then another high-voltage bullet screamed past, but this time grazed Leonor's arm. When the blue electricity nicked her skin, all her senses deadened. "That's your final warning. Drop your weapons or we'll put you down!"

"Hold your fire!" A baritone voice rose from the cluster of guards.

That voice sounded familiar. She searched the cluster for the person behind the voice. Though her vision blurred. Her legs shook. Her body bore the weight of a thousand blabber hoofs. Fire-like tingles electrified her muscles. She glanced at Remedios and slurred her words. "I can't feel my legs."

Leonor's eyes rolled stone white, and she collapsed. Remedios peered down at Leonor lying on the floor. Then landed eyes on the guards. "Shit." Remedios flung her gun to the floor and raised her hands to surrender. "Ride or die," she whispered, as if Leonor could still hear her.

Salvador filtered through the cluster of guards. Clawing his way toward the front line. "Lower your weapons." He lowered a few while they were still aiming for the girls.

Salvador went to Remedios and peered down at Leonor. "The side effects will wear off in a few hours."

"So," Remedios lowered her weapon and stooped to check on Leonor, "does that mean we're free to go?"

"That depends."

Remedios glanced up into Salvador's cloudy eyes.

"Well then, just know Seneca is watching you."

"Thanks, I guess." Remedios scrunched a funny face. "Just so you know, our hearts were never in the death dealing business. We had no choice. But things are going to change in Mafia Land starting today."

"Oh." Salvador laced his fingers, intrigued to know more. "For the better, I hope."

"We could use a little help." Remedios glared at that cloudy eyeball with a side of blue. "We're just kids, you know."

"My door is always open." Salvador gave her a serious eye. "Children are essential for humanity's survival."

* * *

"Zigzags. Tiddle winks. Panda bees. They're all the same," Remedios said playfully. "Now, blabber hoofs. They're something else." She made a screwy face.

"I get panda bees and zigzags. I even get blunder beetles. But what I don't get are orb monkeys. What the hell?" Leonor's eyes beamed and glistened like shiny marbles. "Those have no purpose."

"They're ugly."

"I think they're kind of cute."

Leonor and Remedios glared at Frida.

"Guys," Frida picked up an orb monkey from the dirt, "they eat insects. Lots of them."

"Cute?" Remedios drew closer and peaked at the orb monkey crawling on Frida's palm.

"They slowly absorb the blood of their victims like an aquatic mongrel."

"They're not like aquatic mongrels," Frida whispered. And raised her palm closer to her face. Eyeing the orb monkey. Careful not to scare the little thing.

"Yeah, well." Leonor nudged her head to the left. "Put the orb monkey down so we can finish what we started."

Frida angled her palm. Watched the orb monkey nestle in the dirt again. "That's how it should end."

"How should what end?"

"Everything."

Leonor gave another odd look. "I'm not following?"

"Everything has a purpose, no matter how ugly it may appear at first. Ugly is beautiful. Ugly can be a total Heather. If you look close enough. If you give it a chance." Frida glanced at Leonor. "You know?"

"No," Remedios chimed in. "You don't have to love everything. Sometimes you can't love everything. For whatever reason."

"Look." Frida threw her arms out. "Look how beautiful the world is. The world smells beautiful, too. Have you noticed that? The world can smell beautiful." She tried to lock eyes on Remedios for confirmation. But she was too busy concentrating on kicking pebbles around in the dirt. "The air smells amazing, like fresh juniper." She pointed to the sky. "You've got the clouds, the suns, mountains, insects, flowers, and—"

"Orb monkeys," Leonor said sarcastically.

"Right." Frida's tone was energetic. "It's perfect." She pointed at the dirt. "Nature does not require a leader. It's a perfect system. Everything has a purpose. Nature balances everything. Things go out of whack when you force your will upon it."

"Hey." Remedios locked a curious eye on Frida, then Leonor. "Do you think Mother Saramago will get bored with Seneca and come back?"

"There's nothing for her to come back to," Leonor said. "Now, it's up to us to hone Mafia Land."

"What if we can't?" Frida said. "I mean, look at what happened to the Mothers."

"That won't happen."

"It could happen."

"It won't," Leonor said. "The Mothers never got a fresh start. The Land of Kings ruined what they tried to do." She swirled her finger between Frida and Remedios. "We won't make the same mistakes because we have a fresh start. I hate to say it, but Uncle Stigmata was right."

"You know what?" Frida playfully kissed Leonor's cheek.

Leonor stepped back, a little shocked Frida would dare kiss her. She had killed Königsmarck.

"You're right, we have better odds than they did."

"I know what you guys are going to say. But hear me out," Remedios said. "If it weren't for the Mothers or Stigmata, none of this would be possible."

They gave each other a funny look and continued onward.

A pinprick of light marks the universe's edge. Imperceptible from your vantage point. Someone watches from the other side. Everything is transmission now. A two-lane cosmic highway. You view them, they, you. Though, the person on the other end does not view your light as a pinhole. They see something else—a shimmering light swimming through the murkiness of space—which gives them hope. They see, "land ho!"

— J.S. Nathaniel

J.S. Nathaniel is an American dark fiction author. He writes gothic and dystopian fiction and short stories exploring violence, tenderness, and human darkness.

jsnathaniel.com